My Mother Is a River

Published by Calisi Press in the United Kingdom 2015
Calisi Press, 100 Somerset Road, Folkestone CT19 4NW

www.calisipress.com
info@calisipress.com

ISBN 978-0-9932380-0-0

First published under the original title:
MIA MADRE È UN FIUME
by Elliot Edizioni, Rome 2011
Copyright © 2010 Elliot Edizioni s.r.l.

Translation Copyright © Franca Scurti Simpson, 2015

Cover and book design by:
Charlotte Mouncey, Bookstyle (http://www.bookstyle.co.uk)

This book has been translated thanks to the contribution of a
translation grant awarded by the Italian Ministry for Foreign Affairs

Printed in the UK by TJ International

When I came across My Mother Is a River for the first time, I loved its simple yet powerful story so much that it prompted me to launch Calisi Press to publish it.
I could also recognise the difficulty and frustration of dealing with the devastating disease that dementia is. I know many people who have been deeply affected by this, including some in my immediate family. For this reason I decided that Calisi Press would help raise funds for the Alzheimer's Society and we will donate 50p for every copy of this book sold, at least for a time.

I would like to thank our sponsors –
The Italian Connection, LPA Services and
Terracotta Restaurant – for making this possible.

Franca Simpson
Publisher

Donatella Di Pietrantonio

My Mother Is a River

Translated from the Italian
By Franca Scurti Simpson

To Tommaso and Giacomo,
my two different loves

Some days the illness eats away at her emotions too. The body is listless, it leaks the emptiness that drains it. It loses the ability to feel. It doesn't suffer, it doesn't live, not then.

The check-ups are for my benefit. They reassure me; it wasn't I who made her sick and the progression is slow. Some abilities are partially preserved. I go with her, I look after her, I am a good enough daughter.

The promenade is deserted at this time, and the waves rumble darkly as they break and retreat, grinding up sand and shells. I've parked some way back so that we can walk together a while. My mother walks on her own, but she has slowed down. I link my arm through hers; I can smell the Adriatic Sea on the sleeve of her jacket. On the opposite shore Fioravante, the prisoner, starved on one boiled potato per day.

She relaxes, we fall into step together. I ask her if she likes the smell of the sea. She says, sort of, but she was born in the mountains, she prefers the smell of grass and flowers. She has never stretched out on a beach. It would've been good for her bones, I observe. She laughs. It's too late now, she'd never wear a swimming costume now.

On the other side of the road, the twinkling lights of the restaurants. I suggest a surprise to close our day: let's stop somewhere and eat some fish. No, better not, we're expected for dinner. Another time, I promise.

Your name is Esperia Viola, known as Esperina.

Like a violet, you were born on 25th March 1942, in a house on the border between the districts of Colledara and Tossicia. It was the last house before the mountains, a little stone that had rolled down accidentally on the eastern side of the Abruzzi Apennines.

It belonged to your paternal grandparents, and the families of their two sons were raised there.

Fioravante, the elder, was short, with a large and flat chest, strong arms, a little bow-legged. Look at the photographs. A solid body, made for working the land, or perhaps the land had shaped him so because he had toiled on it since he was a child. What do you think?

He was intelligent and passionate. Look, here you can see his deep black eyes. He was a brawler when he was young. He liked to tell of that time he knifed his neighbour for stealing two fat heifers from the summer pasture. Fioravante then went into hiding for months, hoping the thief wouldn't kick the bucket. He would come down from the woods in the dead of night, and help himself to the bread and cheese his mother had wrapped in a white dishcloth with a blue stripe and left for him on the table before going to bed. He'd breathe in the smell of home and open the bedroom door a crack to reassure himself there were two sleeping outlines in the darkness broken by the starlit window. Then he'd be off again with his mule for company, along the safe paths known only to himself.

He was a hothead, was Fioravante.

You are the daughter of his first leave as a soldier in the war. He came back three times in all. He had married Serafina in October and in February he was already leaving for the front. A fine heifer, he would say to flatter her. Tall, slim and solid, she would stand up straight and graceful in spite of the hard work on the land, with the animals and the housework. And with the girls, later. From the time she had been a little girl she had practised carrying on her head the basket with lunch for the family, digging or harvesting the fields far away. She'd challenge herself to keep it balanced without using her hands when walking on broken ground. You did the same, later on. Your sisters too. There were hardly any mishaps, God help you otherwise. Serafina used to tell the story of how she had once tripped and spilled the macaroni on the grass. She picked everything up and said nothing. Nobody noticed a thing.

Only age eventually forced her into a stoop, sudden and severe, as if all the burdens of her life had descended on her at once, from a great height. It pained her deeply; I think she died of shame. Not just of that, of course, there were a lot of things. But becoming crooked was the final blow to her dignity, always guarded and protected, and reflected in her posture.

You want to know why I'm laughing? Because your mother walked like a model, but if she had to pee outdoors she'd just hike up her skirt, pull her underwear to one side and do it there and then, with her legs apart. Standing up, like a mare. I saw her, I did, really I did. I know she never did that later, but I remember her when she was younger. She understood, later.

Having tracked down the reservist Fioravante to his hiding place and sent him to war, Italy granted him and Serafina, both barely able to read and write, the gift of a postal service. She wrote to him that she was well, and pregnant with a Scialomè, the nickname his family was known by. The real surname didn't count for much, it was only for documents.

Serafina never failed in predicting the sex of her daughters. She just knew. Even with that first boy, she knew, and had cried the whole time, knowing she would lose it. Her womb was a curse for boys. It would welcome them, but wouldn't nurture them for long, and would let them die inside her once they already looked like little boys. She miscarried another after the third girl, and another one after the sixth. Her pregnancies were like that, symmetrical.

How she managed not to perish herself, one of those times, is a mystery. She'd start to bleed, and feel the labour pains come on, then the contractions would expel a nameless and listless tiny body from a womb that was not meant for him. For a few days Serafina would lose appetite and speech, and drink nothing but water and mallow tea, to make up for the tears she'd shed. Then she'd get up and go back to work - that is, she'd get on with life.

To his wife's letter the soldier Fioravante replied with one bearing only a name. She laughed and accepted. Esperia was the gypsy-haired coal woman who, years before, had come for the firing with her brothers and charmed your grandfather's woods with the voice of a sylvan siren. She could bewitch anyone listening, including Fioravante. With that name, he bestowed all that beauty onto his daughter, and you've always sung and whistled the soundtrack to your own life.

You would perform in front of your sisters singing traditional songs, like *Fly Away* and *All the Fountains are Dry*. You can only remember a few verses of *Fly Away*. No, it's not because you've lost your memory, you didn't like the other song, you found it too sad. I can look up the lyrics, if you like. We might even sing a duet, but I'm not as good as you are.

The radio was the second thing to transform your life. I'll tell you about the first another time.

It came when you were sixteen or seventeen, because Fioravante was a shepherd on the foothills of the Apennines and he was poor, but also earnest about Progress. He talked about it all the time, always with a capital 'P'.

He sold some animals and bought it, a battery-operated one at first and then a larger model with a record player. It was pale yellow and brown, with dials on the front and a turntable for the LPs on top, protected by a lid. The world burst into your home. Your own home by now, no longer with grandparents, uncle and aunt and cousins. Too many arguments. Your home, two kilometres away. The radio filled it with whistling and buzzing, and harsh voices, Slavic, Austrian. It was difficult to tune into Italian voices, you had to turn the dials this way and that, ever so slowly, and the next time, the station would be gone. Here were singers and lyrics, you'd learn a song by heart right away and sing it cheerfully. Can you remember any names? Yes, today you can. Luciano Tajoli, Nilla Pizzi, and then Claudio Villa, Domenico Modugno. You loved the Sanremo music festival, it would keep you singing all year round. You also bought records of tragic love stories, lovers star-crossed to their death. Heartbreaking performances over the tones of an accordion. I've heard you sing *Peppino e Rosetta* to the point of exhaustion. I know you're fond of that song, you still try to sing it sometimes, under your breath, don't deny it.

Now, come to the garden with me. Yes, of course it's tomato season, it's August. Let's bring two crates, one for ripe ones, one for green ones. Let's pick one row at a time, you start from the first and I'll start from the last. You fill the yellow crate with salad tomatoes, and I'll fill the blue one with those for sauce. We'll meet halfway and say hello. No, you don't want to do that. Let's do it together then, you pick the green tomatoes, I'll pick the red ones, and we'll be close enough to chat. It doesn't matter if they get mixed up a little, we'll sort them out back in the kitchen. Yes, you told me about Grazietta's garden drying up. Earlier. It doesn't matter.

The father who wanted you Esperina, you first met when you were seven months old. It was his second leave, right on time for the wheat-seeding. And not just for that. On one of those clear November nights your parents conceived Valkiria. And then Diamante on the next leave, another November. The lad would come back from the front horny as a goat, and Serafina's fertility was infallible.

You were born without trouble into the hands of Rosetta, the midwife, who had come from Tossicia on her mule. She was assisted by your paternal grandmother, Clorinda the scornful, and your aunt Palmira, sparingly supportive.

The women from the neighbourhood had come too. They prepared hot water and white linens.

Right after washing you, they shut you for a moment inside the bread chest, and recited a spell to bring you luck.

You were baptised just a few days later, since your brother had died before being blessed. Your legs were wrapped tight in swaddling bands to keep them straight, and for the new mother, chicken broth, forty days' rest from heavy work and no contact with water. They put a *breve* round your neck, a fabric sachet stitched around a fragment of the grindstone from the mill. Palmira took care of that, she was the expert for that sort of thing. Witches came at night time for newborns without one, she said, and sucked their sweet blood, leaving them just before dawn, with bruises and bite marks on their skin. Or worse, they stole them away to their hidey-holes where, once a big fire was lit, they would toss the babies from one to the other over the flames. As morning song broke, tired of their game, they would return them to their cradles, exhausted, and to their unsuspecting mothers.

You girls had a poor childhood, but you never went hungry; the family grew or raised all the food it needed. It was even possible to take in some evacuees, who helped with the work in exchange for food and shelter. They grew fond of the family and after the war, when they came back to visit, they felt the need to stay for a few days, with the excuse that they had come a long way. Raffaele from Roseto, who was only a child at the time, came back as a young man and stayed a week to court Valkiria, until she slapped him in front of everyone and sent him packing.

So Serafina had evacuees at home and a husband at the front. After the third leave, she received only one letter with the name of the new Scialomè she had told him she was carrying, then nothing more.

Fioravante was in Yugoslavia where he'd been taken prisoner by Tito's partisans, that much was known. They gave him one boiled potato a day, often a half-rotten one. He was about to be shot when the wife of one of his jailers recognised in him the Italian who had once rescued her from the brutal attentions of a Fascist squadron. She saved him.

He was freed in a prisoner exchange and, once back on home soil, found the army in disarray. In Trieste an officer told him to go home, that the war was over. He reached Rome and then got from Rome to L'Aquila whichever way he could. He walked from L'Aquila to Montorio, then travelled from Montorio to Colledara on a mule belonging to an acquaintance he had met along the way. He was on foot again for the last few kilometres, cutting through ditches, and collapsed to the ground at near dark in front of the overjoyed snout of his dog Freccia.

He was thirty years old and weighed thirty-five kilos, and some of that was lice, he used to say. He had changed. He was now a communist.

He never stopped admiring Tito for warding off the invaders with no help from the Allies. He didn't get his war pension, some of the necessary paperwork was missing, like his discharge papers.

He never knew foreign land other than as a prisoner. Even the rest of Italy, outside of the Abruzzi, he had only known as a soldier. He had liked Rome. When it was suggested he go on a pilgrimage for the 1975 Jubilee, he indignantly retorted, not for the Pope, I won't.

He didn't get much rest when he came back, he just ate himself back to health and took up his farm work where he'd left off. The war left him with a passion for the world and with malaria, which the pharmacist in Montorio treated with quinine.

After the radio, he was the first in the district to have a television, paid for in instalments. When he wasn't working on the land or in the stable, he'd listen to all the news bulletins. And you girls, not a word, a glance was enough to silence you. Then he'd comment in his own way, swearing and cursing God, the Virgin Mary and all the saints, but in particular St Gabriel of our Lady of Sorrows, the local patron saint. Your mother, who worshipped the saint, considered that the worst sort of blasphemy. Once a year, at the end of the summer, she'd wake you up at dawn, only the older girls, and together you would walk along the path through the woods, to reach the church in Isola del Gran Sasso around midday. There she'd beg forgiveness for that wretched husband of hers, and buy you brooches with the image of the saint looking angelic and thoughtful. And three or four hundred grams of sliced roast pig, to fill the bread she'd brought from home.

It's not a problem, don't worry. I know that when a man comes home tired from work he'd like to find a nice dinner on the table, but I'm sure he can eat something else. This year's sausages are excellent, Auntie's fresh cheese too. If he gets cross, that's his problem. Things have changed, he might as well get used to it. Anyway, it's about time he stopped working as hard as when he was young. We've been telling him for years to keep a cow or two for himself and sell the rest. He's as stubborn as a mule.

So you wanted to cook courgettes with fresh tomatoes and you used cucumbers instead. They look similar, after all. Did he taste them as well? Yes, of course, he trusted you. Yes, I can imagine how disgusting cooked cucumber must be, it's probably bitter and slimy. Even the pigs wouldn't eat it? Anyway, the courgettes are still here, let's cook them now. Once I've peeled them and removed the seeds, I'll slice them thinly. You have already chopped the tomatoes which we now stir into the sautéed onions. Add the basil now. No, not in the garden, there's a pot of it on the patio. Leave it for a few minutes, then add the courgettes and put a lid on it. There's no need to stir so often. Just a minute ago.

There, now we can season it with salt and pepper, a little bit of each. He will then add half a chilli pepper and a fistful of salt to his. Always too much.

Esperine Esperine
your big ears are turning green
your big nose has gone bright red
and it's raining on your head.

Your sisters would jump out from behind a corner, a rock or a fence, to tease you and then run away. Even the sisters born after the war were given unusual names, and all your lives people asked you girls if Viola was your first name. But no, you were Esperina, Valkiria, Diamante, Clorinda, called little Clorinda or Clo to tell her apart from your paternal grandmother, Clarice and Nives. All Viola. Fioravante had named you, each one in turn, with lightning flashes of intuition. Six daughters, he would say, but with pride, while his mother called you silly girls and had eyes only for Palmira and Abele's boys. Yes, your uncle.

You were the eldest, and the shortest. On you fell the greater part of the housework, and you had to be mother and father, with yours busy elsewhere. Tricks and pranks were the order of the day: chilli pepper in the ricotta cheese, a cut-up skirt, salt between the sheets. To this day you still gang up on one another, usually five against one; even your mother would join in at times. Each one has in turn been ostracised by her sisters, sometimes for years. Then, afterwards, sis' here and sis' there. Like when you were children, but it takes longer now.

I remember that Valkiria was the worst. With a name like that, it was inevitable. Tall, beautiful but for the thin and wicked lips, ambitious, full of herself. You used to call her the Boss. She always needed a new pair of shoes and the seamstress, the hell with poverty. When Serafina said no, a mysterious and irreparable hole would suddenly appear on her old dress. No home-woven fabrics for Valkiria, she wanted patterns and sophisticated colours. She refused to go to sewing classes like the others, she wasn't going to wear homemade clothes. If she went too far she'd get a beating from your father, but she would not give in.

She was the only one of his daughters he allowed to ride to Montorio to shop for things that couldn't be found in Colledara or Tossicia. But she was generous and always managed to get a little something for her sisters, after picking out the best for herself. When she climbed onto the saddle, she'd sit still for a minute or two, almost as if to gather herself together before flying onto the battlefield to choose the heroes she would escort to Valhalla. She'd straddle the horse, or ride bareback or side-saddle, depending on the whim of the moment. She appeared magnificent, regal, if you looked at her alone, because the mare Nina, known as the Cripple, was hardly worthy of her.

Valkiria rejected and shamed dozens of young men and then ended up marrying a farmer twenty centimetres shorter than she was, markedly deferential towards her. They had two sons, one a Fioravante, who were sent to boarding school when the parents emigrated to Germany. They used to come back often, because of the boys. On occasions she would issue orders in German, which seemed fitting coming from her. Schnell, schnell!

You lived in a fairy tale and you didn't know it. You were the young shepherdess threatened by the wolf. When the snow drove it to starvation, the wolf of the Abruzzi would leave the woods and wander close to the house in the night, a dark and wary outline on a vast field of light. You could see it from the window, the howling would keep you awake. You shivered with the cold and that ancient human fear. Then the beast would disappear from the window, the glass misted by your fascination, and you'd take refuge in bed, in the warm halo of one of yours sisters.

You herded the flock out to pasture, the goats drove you mad. Sheep graze together under the shepherd's watchful eye. Goats, not caring for rules or anything but themselves, will search out tender shoots on shrubs growing in the steepest, most inaccessible places. Goats will not graze following the crowd and have no respect for property boundaries.

Early in the morning and at sunset, hours of milking would soothe your chapped hands. You'd breakfast on a deep bowl of boiled milk with chunks of bread and a thick slice of curd. You'd sprinkle sugar on top. It was good, but you got bored with it, the same every day.

In June and July wild strawberries were plentiful in the woods, you'd find them by moving ferns out of the way, and transfer them gently to a large leaf twisted into a hollow cone. You'd eat them sitting alone on a rock, scrutinising your scratched legs. Bramble berries darkened in the sun. You'd pick the ripe ones and leave the red ones for tomorrow, the green ones for the following week.

You weren't allowed to count the stars above you, warts would come to afflict the finger you pointed to them with. Perhaps they didn't like children taking liberties with God.

Warts aplenty also if you trapped fireflies in your hands to crush them, trying to discover the secret of their light.

You lived where the wind is born, a bright rugged place, with the mountains in the background. The people were rugged too. Children worked, but not as hard as the adults, which is why in some families they were treated barely better than dogs. Not in your family.

Why do you want to make coffee? We don't drink it. I see, you want to practise because you find it difficult to make. You want to be able to offer it if any visitors come.

Fetch the coffee-maker, it's in the wall cabinet on the right, next to the dish drainer. There is a piece missing, I'll look for it. Let's see, here it is, under the sink, with the detergents, what a scatterbrain you are. No, the water first, up to the valve, then the filter and then the coffee. Screw the top on, I'll tighten it a little for you. Turn the burner on. Not the big one, the little one. Let's ask Grazietta round, your bosom-buddy next door, she likes a coffee in the afternoon. Get the cup ready in the meantime. In the cupboard, the sugar bowl is there too. No, we can't give it to Giovanni just yet.

Our love went wrong, from the beginning. She was too accustomed to sacrifice to allow herself the pleasure of spending time with her baby. Every now and then she'd look up from the ground she was toiling on and towards the bundle she had left under a blanket in the shade of a tree. I was still there. She would have heard a loud cry. She was reassured. She couldn't understand why at night I would ache so much for her attention and play up to get it, while she had all the housework to catch up with after a long day. Besides, those were the orders from her father-in-law and master, when the husband was working away in Germany. Rocco's manner was unbearable, but she could hardly refuse: the hay had to be gathered once dry, the wheat harvested, the animals fed.

The aunties remember me, when I was four or five years old, a crybaby clinging to your apron strings, afraid of being left alone, afraid of storms. A neighbour had once told me that, skinny as I was, the wind could sneak under my skirt and fly me far away, as far as America.

She did love me, but she had other things to do. She was working, for her daughter.

I was not at the forefront of her mind, and I couldn't bear it. Once older, I challenged her version of events, but I didn't really believe her enough. She should've disobeyed, should've loved me in spite of everyone else. Taken my side. And instead the hay had to be dealt with, the ripe wheat and the hungry animals.

Sometimes I relive the memory of wanting to cling to the scent of her, a healthy young woman working the land. Her absence is all that's left of her. My mother was inaccessible, distant. It was not a lack of love, it was haste, just another form of neglect. I'd follow her all the time, some days with the disconsolate pace of a flea-bitten dog, muzzle exuding a quiet desperation. Only at night could I reach her, sliding into her bed. I could smell the tasks of the day on her hair: the cowshed, fresh pecorino cheese, fodder, fried peppers. Again distant, lost in deep sleep, but I was next to her. My breath on the nape of her neck, I'd watch over her a while and then, eventually, fall asleep with my hand in the hollow between her neck and shoulder, where the skin was so soft and pulsating with life.

Some mornings she'd leave early for a field far from home. She'd take me to old Palmantonia, the only neighbour who stayed at home, because she was partly paralysed.

Before leaving she'd hand me a cherry twig, shiny with red fruits dangling among the dark leaves. Some were even in pairs that you could wear like earrings. She had furtively picked it for me from the tree at the bottom of the yard. It was her love token, the promise of her return, consolation for my tears. But not enough for me.

The old woman was not unkind. I was a little scared of her, of the twisted mouth and mismatched eyes, one of which was always watering, the other blinking at regular intervals. She'd try to distract me, but I wouldn't give in. Implacable, I waited for nightfall. The separation would eat away at my heart. I'd let her find me like that, eyes moist with the most recent tears and the twig in my lap, leaves wilted and the cherries one day riper.

Some days I hate her. Like now, driving to her. I hate the time she costs me. When I leave her I am empty, exhausted, my mind blank. I open the car window even though it's cold, to dispel the foulness that overcomes me.

I am incapable of showing her kindness. I never touch her. I can only imagine being able to caress her, her arms, the hands deformed by arthritis, her cheeks, her head. Her hair's started to thin out too, as if the withering at work inside her skull were infecting its very roots. It's like cancer in reverse, it shrivels instead of spreading out. She seems too young for this, she isn't ready. We are not ready.

I don't try to get closer, if I do it feels like the opposing force when you push together the matching poles of two magnets.

I've never put her behind me. I've never forgiven her anything. I was still planning to settle my score with her when she escaped from me into her illness. I quivered with indignation, as if she'd done so to spite me. Or I suspected I'd been the one to push her into it.

I've tried with my partner's mother, fifteen years older and infirm. I bathed her. While we were helping her into the bath, she defecated on its edge. I cleaned up. I soaped her skin, lifting her flaccid breasts to wash the skin folds, where the skin rots and reddens with sweat. Several times, when wiping her anus, the sponge came away foul smelling and streaked with shit. After washing her frizzy, stringy hair, I applied conditioner and then untangled it with a wide-tooth comb. Every now and then she'd slide into the water and I'd pull her up by her armpits. I rinsed her, then Pietro and I got her out of the bath and helped her onto a chair. I rubbed moisturiser on her legs and arms, always so dry. A rivulet of gratitude dribbled from her mouth.

It only tired me a little. I didn't find it the least bit difficult. She is not my mother.

I'm fascinated by the dark channels where the constant craving for my mother vanished, turning into its reverse. The rejection – the fear – of physical proximity. When my turn came, all I was able to return was the emptiness. I look behind us at the network of forking paths. All I can do is tell her the story of her life.

You haven't been well since this morning. You feel as if you have a swollen balloon in your stomach, and yet you haven't eaten. Or perhaps you had something for breakfast, you can't remember. I'll prepare you some bread and olive oil, one slice will be enough. Giovanni is with a school friend, I'll go and pick him up later. Yes, I've seen the photo on the shelf, he looks exactly like Fioravante. He stands with his legs wide open just like his great-grandfather, and with his fists pointing to the ground. It's a shame they never met, they would've liked each other. But Fiore left us early, and Giovanni came late, it can't be helped.

I'll make something for dinner, for you and Dad. Today he's helping Uncle harvest the corn, and tomorrow Uncle will help him. If it doesn't rain. Peppers with chunks of ham, they're a bit rich but you like them. He's playing at a friend's house, I'll go and pick him up later. Shall I tell you a story?

The first thing to turn your life around was school. It was far, in Colledara, one hour's walk along a solitary path which widened a little before the first houses. As well as your satchel, you carried a clean pair of shoes to change into when you got to the village. You'd leave the muddy ones behind a bush to wait for your return. You walked through the dew-moist dawn. In the shaded areas around ditches and under trees, the watery film would outline otherwise invisible spider webs, stretched among the ferns. You didn't feel the weight of a butterfly that would for an instant conceal itself on your hair. Where the ground was soft, you'd hop from one stone to the next.

It amused you to walk for long stretches with your eyes closed, sure as you were of the path. You could recognise where you were from a smell, from a sound, from how the sun faded on your skin when you entered the beech wood. Frogs would be splashing by the pond, and the uncovered root of an oak would try to trip you up by the bend before Heifer's Ditch. One morning you did fall on your face and turned up to class with a torn skirt and cut hands. That taught you to cheat, and from then on you'd keep your eyes half-closed to judge distances.

Fioravante was keen on you girls going to school. He never bought you a toy, but books, yes. *Heart*, *Pinocchio*, *Don Quixote*, and girly novelettes.

In winter it was impossible to walk the distance to school. You could stay in the village with Aunt Dirce or with Marianere, a family friend. You preferred the latter because your aunt looked like an ogre's wife. You'd reappear in the yard with the good weather, as the sun slipped behind Mount Camicia and the animals trudged back to the stable with their heads down. Your sisters would shriek with joy, the bickering would come later.

Your teacher adored you. A world that spoke Italian was now open to you. And you lost the naivety of your situation as you learned from your school friends how different their lives were from yours. After lunch you observed children playing hide and seek in the narrow streets, discreetly watched by mothers at the windows.

In spring, you managed to get home just in time to take the sheep and goats for their afternoon grazing. Of course, you'd have your lunch first. Speaking of which, would you like some more bread and oil?

One after the other the sisters started going to school. Voices, laughter and screams would be heard along the path and the frogs would splash into the pond well before you reached it. After school you'd argue about whether or not you should return home or stay and sleep over at Marianere's: night time in the village was a diversion Valkiria was not willing to give up and she was given to weather forecasts that were as fanciful as catastrophic, to discourage even the most reckless among you girls. If she were the only one to stay behind she'd risk being taught a lesson by her father, who thought her lazy.

She's sleeping as if she'd been listening to a fairy tale. She breathes with her mouth open, wheezing softly at regular intervals. She'll be disorientated when she wakes up, she'll think it's morning, or that she's staying with me. Then she'll recognise the old sofa and slowly realise she's home and, perhaps, that it is afternoon. I don't know what dreams startle her. I watch her closely. She has the sorrowful expression of a not-quite-full moon. The skin is thinning over her nose, her cheekbones. It's stretched and shiny, as if about to break. She could be dead.

Her body's ageing rapidly, mirroring the decline of her mind. She used to run down the stairs, whistling. Now she grabs the rail with her right hand and increasingly strains to lift her weight from one step to the next.

There are a few blessed moments, when she seems unfettered, as if returned to herself. In truth she's collapsing, right under our disbelieving eyes. Some of her teeth have broken. She has that face like a sorrowful moon.

She turns over on the sofa with a moan. Her mouth works as she summons some saliva, and finally closes. Her breathing settles, only her chest is working, now, and her eyes beneath the eyelids.

A ray of sun falls through the window on her hand. Her knuckles and veins are swollen. The last segment of each finger abruptly changes direction at its axis, as if shunted towards the thumb by a sudden gust of wind. On her ring finger the effect is so marked that it might have been broken and badly set. Her wrist is swollen too. I look to myself to figure out if I am the monster who's allowed all this to come to pass.

I drag my attention away from her sleep and walk around the rooms with the vague purpose of tidying up. She used to be so exacting about tidiness, and tried to impose that on me, without success.

Now there are packs of pasta and sugar, some sealed and some open, among the crystal stem glasses and the coffee sets in the display cabinet. I return them to their rightful place, only to find insect spray. I move that to the cupboard under the sink and there I find bottles of vinegar and oil among the detergents.

We could do with a mathematical model to tidy this house, to be applied once or twice a week. If something's missing you've no idea where to look, and then you come across something you were looking for days ago. I found the salt in the freezer.

I open the fridge to get a drink: there's a lidded saucepan on the top shelf. For an instant I hope she might have prepared something different for dinner than tomato sauce, the oil and basil usually forgotten. I slowly lift the lid. It's empty.

Let's play, today I am a Latin teacher. Let's test Esperia Viola on Phaedrus' *Lupus et Agnus*, which you knew so well. Let's have it.

Ad rivum eundem lupus et agnus venerant, siti compulsi.
Superior stabat lupus, longeque inferior agnus. Tunc...

That's enough, you've done well. What are you complaining about? You used to know all of it and now only the beginning. I don't even know that.

And so, young lady, you went to secondary school. During the school year you'd stay in Atri with your paternal grandparents, who'd bought a little house in the country, with some land around it. So that their grandchildren could study too, he'd say. The boys, she'd specify. But they never amounted to much.

Years later, with your second family, you would retrace that scant migration towards the Adriatic Sea, enough to change the life of farmers like yourselves.

Clarice wanted to join you. Ill-fated Clarice, as you sisters referred to her when she wasn't there. But when you were cross she was Boiled Face. "Ugly Boiled Face, who's gonna want you?" you girls would spit out to her, without mincing your words. If Serafina had heard you, though, she would've smashed your faces in herself.

So Clarice spent a year with you, her married sister now moving down the valley. Everybody happy, on both sides, and I the happiest of us all.

I was ten years old and had a blue school smock tailored by the seamstress, with my initials embroidered by hand. I thought it was my best outfit, while my school mates couldn't wait to take it off, some mornings pretending to have soiled it with their milky coffee so that they could show off a new top. I'd watch the teacher open her mouth, fearing she would let us off having to wear it and instead she'd insist we wear it after breakfast. I am sorry, I'm talking about me now, not you. I felt so different from my school mates. And you? You too, a little.

You liked the school in Atri, but in June you couldn't wait to go back to your home in the mountains, to your meagre certainties.

I know that she was instead going back to a brand-new sort of anguish. The bad boy who had fantasised about the body of Esperia the coal woman, saw her again through ogre eyes in her namesake, barely more than a child. With his stiff limbs, he would force her against a sun-warmed wall when she came out of a pen, and he would rub against her the erection hiding in his rough cloth trousers. He touched her, fondled her. She could feel the acid breath of pecorino on her face. She'd twist her mouth, turning her face towards the lizards sprinting over the stones, while the cat strolled by indifferently. She managed to get away every time, escaping the brutal hands and running in tears to her mother.

There was no irreparable damage. Serafina kept an eye out and protected her, trying to ensure that at least one of the sisters was with her firstborn at all times. She comforted her and tried desperately to keep the family together. For the beast, only a few words: leave the girl alone. The last time she said it, it was through gritted teeth, a knife to his throat. The one for slaughtering the pig.

Esperina's memories are fading, I'm allowed to edit her story. She spoke of the harassment suffered at her father's hand only once, when I was already grown up and he'd been dead for years. She let me love him, when I was a child and a teenager. I was his favourite grandchild, the first grandchild, he would say in Italian.

When she told me, she was unusually concise, dry. I could feel the catch in her throat, the effort to hold back the tears. I never said a word. After a while she repaired to a trivial subject, with her usual squandering chatter.

I thought about it sometimes, if I had reasons to doubt her misfortune. I had none. Other than the disloyal, obstinate determination to hang on to my wonderful Grandpa Fioravante, who carried me in his arms to pick figs.

I've searched for a link between that abusive love and the half-mother she later became. She deprived me of loving gestures, cuddles, caresses. Her hands were hard, they touched me rarely and briefly, in the efficient ministration of care, with rare affectionate lingering. As if tending to the lambs.

I wanted a reason to forgive her. I tried to imagine a young woman driven to hold herself back with her own baby because of the memory of the shameful ordeal she had endured, still fresh on her skin. It was her way to respect her, to protect her. It was her way to love her. Hers was a love in reverse, she held herself back for fear of loving too hard, so that her child wouldn't feel like prey, as she had done.

I don't know if this is true. I wanted a reason to forgive her. We've never settled our differences. All my life I have searched for her, feeling like a beggar. I'm still searching for her. I can't find her. I look for her. Mother of sorrows.

The mountain crumbles. It is soft and porous, and over time freezing water expands in the crevices and the rock cracks. The shattered pieces roll down the slopes and collect into heaps.

Aristide of Tanganelle had opened up a quarry, nobody quite knew where. Not on our side. You could hear the bang of explosives from time to time, and then a deep rumble shuddering the entire body of the mountain, unfurling through the whole range, amplified by the echo in the valley. The animals would stir. Then it seemed that even more rocks would fall, but it was only an impression. Stones would turn up everywhere. They infested the few arable fields skirting the wood. The plough would move forward with a clatter of iron hitting stone, and lost its edge.

Once a year you'd go hunting for stones with the others. Nobody does that any longer. You'd wrench them off the planet's crust, which had already assimilated them, and carry them to a mound in the middle of the field. The land could finally be ploughed, but within a few months it would fill up again, as if by magic. The mound grew over time, providing a home for lizards, a few snakes. Brambles would grow around it, and then, later, over it. It was a minute ecosystem. Children wanted to go stone-picking when the blackberries were ready, so that they could gobble up the berries, but also use the overripe ones as paint. You girls would draw family portraits on the flat faces of the stones: Fioravante with a handlebar moustache, Clo with sticking-out ears and you with your bushy hair. Then you pretended they could talk and even made them fight, smashing them against each other. They were your puppets. Occasionally someone's finger would pay the price. The nail on Nives' right index finger turned a blackberry colour and fell off. It grew back later, it's true, but a little out of shape.

Shall we make a list of other jobs no one does any more?

Homemade soap: pig fat and caustic soda, in a large copper cauldron. Children had to be kept away to avoid burns. That's how Clarice's face was lost.

Doing the laundry at the river: tablecloths, sheets, with the soap we have just mentioned. Once in June and again in September, that's why girls needed well-stocked trousseaus. You ended up bathing yourselves too, blinded by the sun bouncing off the water's surface. For small washing you went every day to the district fountain.

Washing sheep, before shearing: again in the river, dipping them in turns in a deep enough bay for a vigorous rub.

Weeding wheat: in May, when the plants were still green, you'd be criss-crossing the field pulling out weeds, being ever so careful not to tread on the stalks already bearing hairy, unripe sheaves.

You tell me one now. You can't think of anything. I'll help you. Still talking of wheat, what did you have to do before taking it to the mill? No, after threshing. Wash it, yes. And then it'd be spread over large coarse canvas sheets to dry in the sun, children guarding it from the poultry's insatiable curiosity. Talking of hens, it's time to collect the eggs. Let's see if you remember where they lay them. Later we'll break them for a potato omelette, Giovanni loves that.

She never forgets my son. He spent a lot of time with her when he was little. When I came home, breathless and anxious to see him again, the signs of their attachment would send spasms of resentment through me. At times, after a first hug, the child would still want to stay with his grandmother. Come back to mummy, she'd let slip occasionally. I corrected her with ruthless precision, looking her straight in the eye, silently challenging her, don't even try. I strived to keep her in her place, so she wouldn't take him away from me.

She had announced during my pregnancy that she wished to compensate me for her once-distant mothering by becoming a full-time granny. Perhaps she wanted to make it up to herself as well as me, for what we'd missed. I had to keep her at bay. Finding the excuse that she had too much to do at home, I replaced her over time with nursery school. She'd still see the child, of course, but not every day. After a time, the first symptoms of the illness.

Giovanni arrived on winter solstice night, on the cusp between Sagittarius and Capricorn. Sleet lashed at the windows. We had wanted to welcome our child by ourselves, Pietro and I. When I asked him to call my parents, the nurses were already washing the baby.

Later, my mother insisted on staying at the hospital to assist me. Wrapped in the flowery green shawl that Nives had given her, she slept in the armchair in the corner, tired after a day that had seemed to be ordinary until the end. She was so tired she snored, and didn't hear me when I called to her in a whisper, so as not to disturb the other new mum. She got up once to offer me a glass of water. I spent the night writing her a letter in my mind, which I then forgot. I shivered, with the rage and cold I felt at that inconsiderate sleep, the consummate skill in being both intrusive and distant. I was indignant at the way she'd spoiled the moment by making me notice, when she was barely through the door, that my nightdress and sheet were stained with blood and needed changing. I'll never tell her, not like that.

Just before dawn I was overcome by my love for her, obstinate and hateful, guilty of not having found its way to hers.

I feared for my baby. I didn't deserve him, not with my wicked thoughts. He looked fresh from the angel factory, his head fragrant as bread, his breath of warm milk, big eyes already open to the world.

The pig has to die in winter, when the cold stills the dawn and slices your face. When the frost is like crystal and the moon is bright. Then early one morning, yesterday's puddles cracking under your steps, you might be surprised by the cry of the beast being killed somewhere in the valley, on the slope of a hill, where smoke rises ahead of sunrise.

When you're near, the death cry always sounds louder and sharper, it drives the silence from the valley, then starts to shrink, to become raspy. It drowns in blood, rattling with the final tremors of the large body.

The pig perhaps knows it is the end: at other times during the short year of its life it will be removed from the sty to be weighed or castrated, but it will never shriek as uncontrollably as when the time has come to slaughter it. The men push it, they pull it, grabbing its ears and tail, and the beast just digs in its hooves, shrieking and shaking its head.

The pig is blessed, protected by St Anthony. That was the only meat you ever ate: a chicken at Christmas, Easter and special occasions. Never veal, but pork, yes, every family would slaughter at least one for the winter. When I was as young as Giovanni is now, it was a real party, a day of plenty, a feast day. All the relatives would come, they'd be offended if you didn't ask them, and if you did, they'd end up eating a quarter of the animal.

Nothing's wasted, starting with the blood, collected as it spurts from the gash in the throat, bright red, warm and throbbing. Once cooked it becomes black pudding, sweet or savoury, with onions. Hardly anyone does that any more, they say that it's revolting. The surplus of lard was a comfort, an abundance at home, where olive oil would run out in the spring and you didn't even know what butter was.

On the morning of the slaughter you take what's necessary to prepare the meal of the day. The brain is fried with dry chilli peppers and garlic cloves. It's a dish reserved for those who've done the killing, they eat it standing up, as a starter, waiting to sit down at the table. In the meantime the two cleaned halves of the animal are hung to rest in a cold room. The rind now looks like freshly shaved skin. The women cook pasta and, for the second course, *cif-ciaf*, a stew with or without tomato sauce, a simple dish with bay leaves, chilli pepper, and garlic in its skin. The special flavour comes from the freshly butchered meat. After even a day or two it wouldn't taste the same. You must taste the recently departed life.

The men eat and drink, then play cards and *morra*. They toast the pig, *death to you and health to those who feast on you*. They are neighbours, they do the rounds to kill the brothers, that's what they call the pigs sometimes.

After forty-eight hours the cold has done its job and the carcass is rigid, ready to be butchered, broken. Women must not be menstruating, otherwise the lot will go bad. Whoever believes that these days? You've never believed that, I know.

The work started early in the morning, right after tending to the animals and having breakfast, perhaps fried eggs and bacon with dry peppers. The hams are carved out, as roundly as possible. You have your secret way.

Before storing them in vats under salt, you'd press them hard to squeeze the residual blood out of the larger vessels. Blood can spoil the meat.

Your hams are good, but they make you thirsty. If you promise not to tell you-know-who, I'll confess that I buy Parma ham for home, it's sweeter. What do you mean, why shouldn't you tell him? He'd be affronted, he raises his pigs like children.

Dad rolls the loins, already salted and washed with wine, on a bed of crushed pepper. He pats them all over to make the powder cling to the surface. He sneezes non-stop, blessing himself. Finally he stuffs the meat in the casing and ties it firmly. He trusts no one, he takes care of it himself.

The waste cuts are tasty: tail, shanks, ears and snout. A little of the lard, what isn't needed for cooking or soap, is thrown away.

By now night has fallen, you are tired. Nothing remains of that large carcass. The men go to sleep. For days the smell of raw meat lingers around the house and drops of fat fall from sausages hanging from sticks, when the flames burn brighter on the hearth.

In a few weeks, all those who don't have a sow will buy two little curly-tailed pink piglets, and a new pig year will begin. Over four seasons they'll be reared to sacrifice, so we can have another day like this.

The pig is a godsend. When you don't have the time, or the inclination, when you've forgotten to make dinner, you can just get something from the cellar. You wait a moment to let your eyes adjust to the half-light and there they are, in neat rows on the shelves, the cans and wide-mouth jars with sausages preserved in oil that congeals to green in the cold. Or you might look up and decide to cut down a loin hanging from a string or even pull down a ham from the iron hook and start on that, once and for all.

The garden is another lifesaver. At this time of year it's like a supermarket, all you have to do is reach out and grab something. The peppers are sick, you say. They start to rot at the tip and then, slowly, the decay rises towards the stalk. And this year's melons, only the winter ones are good, the other ones taste like medicine. Bread comes in handy too, of course. Bread and oil. Bread and tomato. Bread and pork.

You became a woman on your own. You'll bleed from down there, your mother had warned you, opening the drawer in the bedside table where the towels were kept. You took some with you to Granny Clorinda's house, in Atri.

You waited a long time, knowing that the other girls at secondary school had already started with that business. And they had boobs, hips, bums, slender waists. The older boys would look and try their luck. And you were a little girl, slight, a little stooped even though you were short, your eyes big and frightened. And that was one of the things that frightened you: your periods were keeping you waiting. On your ribs, two hard buttons that hurt, tender to the touch. You spied on them obsessively, searching for a hint of swelling, growth, explosion. You used to dream of waking up with breasts. Your hand explored the insignificant little hair in your armpits. Not your pubis, you mustn't do that.

Finally the blood came, one summer afternoon. Serafina showed you how to fold a linen towel to reach a sufficient thickness, and how to fix that to your pants with a safety pin. Then she left you to your happiness and your cramps. Coming in waves, each would reach an insufferable climax, then decrease while another had already started to rise elsewhere. You remained crouching on the grass, holding tight onto a stick pointing to the ground, your white knuckles wrapped around it. The sheep came close to look at you, grazing around you. Red streaks dribbled down your legs from the saturated cloth. You reached for a leaf to stop the drip, following its path in reverse. Or you'd watch it dry with restrained dread, until you got to use the water in the basin back home. The dogs would come and sniff you, their snouts prying between your legs.

You were now old enough to attend the neighbourhood dances. Families with young sons and daughters would arrange two lines of chairs on opposite sides of a large room, cleared for the occasion. The boys would sit on one side and the girls on the other. An accordion was needed, and food and drink. Between one dance and the next the girls of the host family walked among the guests with trays clinking with glasses, or laden with bread and oil, ham, big homemade biscuits. You're right, the women weren't offered wine, only water. Daughters must be escorted by at least one parent, who would make sure the boys' hands stayed where they should and safe distances were respected. There was hardly need for that, the dances were so fast – waltz, polka, mazurka and *saltarello* – they didn't allow any impudence, they were just enough to excite the young men's interest. To get to know you, yes.

The accordionist, with the aid of some Montepulciano d'Abruzzo, would work the air inside the bellows and the mood of the party. If he was young the girls would buzz around him, but he couldn't dance. When the instrument started, the boys stood up and crossed the room, with a nod to the chosen one who would then take the extended arm. You could smell garlic on their breath and sour old sweat on their armpits. Why are you laughing? I know how it was, you made me go sometimes, it was still the way. Go on, laugh, it was so embarrassing for me, a committed secondary-school student. Serves you right, you're laughing so hard your stomach hurts. I was always the last to be asked and, if there were more girls than boys, I'd be left standing. I don't know, because I was so skinny and looked so scornful, I suppose. No, it didn't please me, I felt twice insulted.

But you yearned to go. You'd even rub your teeth with sage before leaving the house. As for Valkiria, that's another story. She'd parade in her high heels and fancy bell-shaped skirt with matching sweater and cardigan. They call that a twin-set these days, can you believe it. It's true, she was the queen of the ball. She stood out from all the others and overshadowed her partner, taking the lead, but they all wanted to have at least a turn with her.

At the end of the party the air was thick with vaporised sweat, smoke, and spirits let free, an overheated humanity condensed under the blackened ceiling. Someone would go and look at the sky outside and assess the position of the moon. They'd come back in, the smell of the cold lingering on their coat, saying let's go. Dawn and the animals' first feed just a few hours away.

I hated them when they made me take part in the tribal rites, as I called them. I was the female on display for males biologically old enough to reproduce. I hated being chosen in that way, and that it was her in particular, a woman herself, who made me submit to the customs of that wretched world. She was ahead of all that, more open-minded, but subdued by obligations and duties.

A rebel under pressure, I'd fight back with hostility. I would distance myself, thinking about the next day, when I would read a French poem, addressing my soft Rs to a hushed classroom.

The lack of affectionate attention from my mother didn't trouble me at that time, or it did so in yet unknown ways. That's when I stopped yearning for her. I looked away from her. Only the night before a maths test would I go back to sleep in her bed.

Something else was distressing me at the time. Her almost sudden need to control me, her pressing anxiety. As if I'd escape her forever, unless she could change me overnight. I was already gone, and she didn't know it. She chose that time to guide me, in a frenzied, overbearing way. She'd start softly, but when I felt her breathing down my neck I would automatically contradict her, and she'd become entrenched in her trivial demands to clean the bathroom and wash the dishes. We fought about the housework, the age-old clash between mother and daughter embittered by our shared history. Just to disobey her, I'd go and help with the harvest, gather the hay, dig, even. I'd choose to break my back on jobs I wasn't ready for, with my father's puzzled complicity. I'd clean the cowshed – pushing enormous wheelbarrow-loads of fragrant shit – but not the kitchen. On my return to the yard, I'd stand up to her thundering gaze from the truck loaded with freshly gathered grass. My father would turn the engine off. And her: *get those weeds out of your hair*.

I refused to learn how to make homemade pasta or bread. I can't sew the hem on a pair of trousers, but I can drive a tractor. Esperina is always talking about women my age who can keep a clean house and are quick about it, because they also work at the Minerva factory. She doesn't care much for my established professional practice.

I have to go and see her every two or three days. I can't bear longer separations, I'm scared I might lose her. I imagine that she might deteriorate suddenly, like Rita's mother who shat on the landing one morning, and then sat down next to it, waiting. Or like old Lisetta, who'd pull out clumps of her hair and hide them in the spaghetti with tomato sauce.

I run upstairs, push the door wide open and look quickly around me to reassure myself that the kitchen and living room are more or less as they should be. I must believe I can control the evolution, the involution. After a superficial inspection, I open the oven, the dish drainer, the fridge, then move to the bedroom and start on the drawers. I find dirty underwear with the ironed vests.

Today we're going to work together. Nothing difficult, don't worry. I know you like it better when I tell you stories, but the things in your bedroom drawers are a bit mixed up, we'd better sort them out.

Do you remember how untidy I was when I was younger? No, not when I was a little girl, later, we'd start fighting the moment you walked into my room. How we quarrelled over that. I wouldn't tolerate intrusions into my territory and you couldn't forgive me the mess. Once, to punish me, you didn't let me go to a student party, where I could've danced the shake, never mind the mazurka. I'd worked hard for a whole week to get Dad to agree. I didn't speak to you for three days, and didn't eat a thing. Not quite, really, I did peck a little bit behind your back, when you weren't looking. I even dribbled bleach on the flowery skirt you'd given me for my birthday, it was very fashionable in those days, worn with wooden clogs and the leather bag with the Vera Tolfa etching. You asked Aunt Clarice to dissuade me from retaliating, she came on purpose to get me to start eating again. I couldn't say no to that little boiled face.

Look, I've brought some sticky labels. I'll write the contents of the drawers on them and then we'll stick them on. This way, when you put away clean clothes, you can read and not mix things up.

SUMMER TOPS on the first drawer, and WINTER TOPS on the second one, which is deeper. One of the handles is broken, we'd better replace it.

I know this house inside out. Near the chimney there is a chipped tile, the big cauldron fell on it, the one for making tomato sauce at threshing time. Twenty years ago, I think. There were many people working, we rustled up two kilos of spaghetti with garlic and olive oil.

In my old bedroom the rolling shutter sticks in a particular place, it must not be rolled down completely. The bath tap tells the time, drip by drip, it's left a streak of limescale on the pink bottom. Clashes are forgotten, neglect and dust render all surfaces alike, dulling already faded colours. Charred fat hardens on the burners with each use, becoming darker and more difficult to remove.

I resist. I call the plumber, I buy cleaning products. I sweep, dust, rub, wash the floor. I clean the fridge and this time I find a solitary lid on the middle shelf. I diligently continue to show her how to use the dishwasher I bought her last year, all that's needed is for her to press a button. She insists that washing a few plates by hand is quicker, but she just wipes them with a sponge and leaves them to dry without rinsing.

I look around me through my mother's eyes. The house becomes alien, hostile. It hides things, it plays tricks, it's not safe. A malignant force inhabits it, creating disorder and telling her to do strange things. Where to put this clean saucepan in her hands? The fridge's light welcomes her, the humming always familiar. Here are the eggs, in rows of six, like toy soldiers. You can't be mistaken, nothing else can be placed in those shapes, but you might forget which are the fresh ones and which are not. Which is the row for today's eggs? The first or the last? While she thinks of that, she leaves the saucepan to rest next to the cheese.

I no longer trust the eggs. I will only use them for Giovanni if I've just picked them. The order in the drawers will last a week at most.

Even her body feels alien. She can't remember if it's eaten, if it needs washing. Every day she discovers with unfailing wonder the second toe of the right foot, which has been raised for years, overlapping the big toe. She will wear a woollen jumper on a stifling August morning. She doesn't know she's hot.

All sorts of things go on inside her head. She usually reports pain, but more and more often a burning on one side, where she was hit many years ago by a beam. She moves strands of hair aside to show me that the growth there is less dense. It comforts her to think that the old injury is the cause of all that ails her. Sometimes she describes her head as an ants' nest, then she reads dismay in my eyes and says again don't worry.

She tells me of a fire burning right where she's pointing with her misshapen middle finger, and invites me to feel for myself the spot where the large beam hit her. The spark starts there, and for a few minutes the flame is as small as that of a match, the heat strong and contained. She pauses, eyes closed, mouth clamped tight. Suddenly the fire blazes like a scorched prairie sprinkled with petrol. She mimics the explosion of the blaze: WHAM! She asks me why. I feel my mouth move soundlessly, searching for a plausible answer. I desist.

I look at her poor confused head and hope that at least the ants will be consumed in the fire.

You fell in love with Cesare, my father. How could you? He's your cousin! You barely knew each other, that's how. He lived down the valley, several kilometres away, through country paths. It all started with a dance where you found each other again, suddenly grown up and attractive. There were other dances, and each time you'd arrange a dubious, secret meeting, by the stream, the beech wood or at Acquasanta.

At home you'd say you had to go and fetch rennet or starter yeast from Tubbiole, and you'd escape to the appointed place. Or he might surprise you on the pasture beneath Pietralunga, the eastern flank of Mount Camicia. Fioravante once surprised you both, swooping down on you on his way to mark the lambs while you two were snuggling together on a rock, deep in conversation. Your Ulysses managed to escape just in time, diving among the flock and moving quickly from sheep to sheep, while you distracted Polyphemus, answering that "Nobody" was there.

Your love was opposed and questioned just enough. The issue of the blood relationship was raised but wasn't deemed to be important. Cesare was the eldest son of Maria Concetta, Serafina's sister. The families were compatible as far as history and attitude to work went. The two patriarchs tried to come to an understanding, but they were each more stubborn than the other, both with the same foul temper on them, according to your mother. The same they were not: Fioravante, a communist dictator, I'd say, to Rocco's fascist one.

No, I won't take the melon back with me, we still haven't eaten the one I brought back yesterday.

Once he'd got his uncle's reluctant blessing, Cesare could come to your house, to "talk". He'd come after dinner, earlier sometimes. In winter you ate at six, and then you would both sit on two chairs next to each other in a corner by the chimney, talking quietly as the hours stretched kindly into the darkness. Across the floor, Fioravante nodded off, his chin on his chest and a half-closed eye like a sly old cat. Your sisters would dash out of the room to which they'd been confined, sniggering and giggling. Nives needed a drink every ten minutes. Only a lit candle would remain on the cleared table, while the glare of the flames you fed from time to time with more wood made your cheeks glisten, and sparkled in your eyes and smile. Your father would stir in his sleep, mumbling. You'd both move your legs to ward off pins and needles, you always composed and with your knees together, mind, because you were wearing a skirt.

No, I won't take the melon, we still have the other one.

It would get late. Serafina had taken Fioravante's place in the chair for her watch, her mouth opening in sleep and pointing to the sky, her sewing in her lap. In all their lives they never had a sofa. Her head was subject to occasional instability, abruptly subsiding downwards or sideways with noisy inhalations, and then settling again for a time. And you two kept on talking, whispering now, by the weakening flame.

You'd suddenly realise it was late, Cesare would stand up and wish his aunt goodnight by talking into her ear, startling her awake. A few times she pricked herself with the needle. Then your hero would open the door to a cruel moon and set off on his return journey. You could see him walking down the icy path while you put out the dying fire.

56

No, I won't take it with me because I have another one at home we haven't eaten yet.

You got married on the 27th of December 1960. You had to get a special dispensation from the Church because of the blood tie.

Fafina, the seamstress, stitched you a simple dress, just under the knee, and a white coat. You went to Montorio for the shoes and handbag, also white. A few nights earlier, friends, neighbours and the Scialomè relatives came to your father's house for a reception, to deliver the presents. A few days later, the same thing at the groom's house. Sets of crockery and glasses for him, for you items for the trousseau, listed by Nives in an inventory to hand to your barely literate mother-in-law. I found it again, look, at the bottom of a drawer. Blankets, five, sheets, ten sets, sanitary linen towels, incredibly, one hundred, enough for a lifetime of periods. That's how it was. Families would push themselves from hardship into misery, so as not to lose face with their in-laws. Not Serafina, though, she was careful, and it was her sister, after all. You'd asked your mother-in-law round one Sunday to see the trousseau spread over your parents' big bed, frilly all over with white handkerchiefs tied in little bows. Also bedecked with bows were the live lambs and chickens for the couple's families, and the baskets overflowing with all sorts of goodness, brought by relatives to restore larders depleted by the celebratory dinners given before the wedding.

Not even the mare that carried you on the path from the house to the open road, her back covered with the good cape, escaped your sisters' bow flurry. Waiting for you was a bus hired for the occasion, which then proceeded to Colledara and Tossicia to pick up guests along the way. Even on that day Fioravante ended up cursing, because the trousers tailored by the famed artisan in Colledara turned out to have one leg shorter than the other, and had to be cut to even them out. He said that the Lord had made him whole, and the tailor maimed him.

You were beaming, waving at people from the window. It's not true that all brides are beautiful.

In Tossicia, at eleven o'clock, in the incense-scented church of Saint Sinforosa, don Emilio was ready for you, and you were soon standing at the altar. Cesare was trying to calm down by clenching his teeth to stop his jaw muscles from throbbing. From the alcove by the second column on the left of the central nave, the fifteenth-century reclining Madonna stared at you, stunned in her wooden fixity. Dedicated to the Divine Providence, she didn't know she would be stolen and then found again, in a London street market, years later.

You turned your head back with a quick motion of the neck towards the first pew, where your parents and sisters sat. One was missing. She was at the back, in the darkest corner, hiding her misfortune from the world and from the God who had not protected her from fire. Only for a moment did she regret not dying. Serafina, her eyes anxiously looking around for her, felt something missing from her heart. But Clarice didn't move, she hid all the way through to the go-in-peace, so as not to spoil the ceremony.

After the photograph in front of the church, marked by that same absence, the bus took everybody back to the bride's house. Well, as far as it could. Nina the Cripple, faithful mare, had been waiting for hours, grazing on the sparse grass and trying to shake off those big white flies that her mistresses Valkiria and Clorinda had tied to her tail and ears that morning.

Scare-the-devil Maria, cook to the big banquets in the area, had been working for two days on the bridal feast, aided by the women of the house and some of the neighbours. In the absence of fridges she preferred to work in winter, obsessed as she was with her fear of maggots infesting the meat. She repeatedly instructed her helpers to cover all food, cooked and raw, with clean old tablecloths. She carefully guarded a bundle containing those ingredients she wouldn't find in the farmers' houses: butter, mozzarella, anchovies in oil, parmesan cheese and a few mysterious spices. She used lavish quantities of pepper.

For you she had prepared an appetiser of cured meats, pecorino cheese from your home and flower-shaped fritters. A mutton stew followed, scented with rosemary, and it was on a fragment of bone in the sauce of that very dish that Diamante broke her already rotten upper front tooth. She would spend the rest of the afternoon with a hand in front of her mouth.

The main courses started with the traditional egg stracciatella in chicken broth, immediately followed by the boiled meat. Then came a heavy red timbale made with chicken giblets, mozzarella, hard-boiled eggs and parmesan. Finally, tagliatelle with a ragout of mixed meats, served later with peas.

Once the prescribed pasta was devoured, everybody got up to watch Vittorio Giuviddi's customary challenge to himself. He always managed to gobble three portions of pasta at any banquet people dared invite him to, but that time he surpassed himself with four. Because this feast was better than any other, he explained to his laughing supporters.

After each course, you walked among the guests to thank them, asking if they liked the food, making sure there was enough bread and wine on the table. You might dash to fetch a carafe of water. And you chatted, chatted with everyone, so happy you forgot to eat. Cesare got tired of following you around and, after the roast lamb and potatoes, he surreptitiously caressed your cheek and took off to an empty room to play cards with his friends.

It was dark by the time the one-hundred-egg cake made it to the table, with the double filling of custard cream and chocolate sauce, soaked with Alchermes and maraschino cherry liqueurs.

Depleted by the unusual abundance, your relatives took away whole portions of timbale and leftover meat and, in separate bundles, slices of cake for the rest of their families, for the days to follow. In their pockets, five sugared almonds from Sulmona wrapped in tissue paper, something your mother didn't want her firstborn's wedding to be without.

You lived with your parents, the first two years. I was born one sleety February afternoon, in the hands of the same midwife, Rosetta, who had come from Tossicia on the back of another mule. Cesare was disappointed, he'd wanted a son, and wouldn't see me for three days. Then he glanced in the crib and fell in love with that tiny little mouth, so he said. As a teenager, when struggling with the shadow of a moustache, I always blamed him for wanting me to be a boy. And why ever did you swaddle me? I should've been able to kick my legs about. Absolutely, I had to! They made you, to prevent bandy legs. But after six weeks you noticed that, instead of crying as I had done before, I glared at you, and you never did it again.

I was a doll for your younger sisters. They'd come back from school every day, even when it was wet and windy, just to cuddle me. When I got fed up with being passed from one to the other to shrieks of GIVE HER TO ME GIVE HER TO ME, I would scratch their faces.

How do I remember it all? You told me, many years ago.

The black-clad countrywoman guards the grazing sheep.

She's let them into the vineyard, among the rows; they'll do no harm in October, and will enjoy the sweet surprise of the few grapes that escaped harvest. It's late, the woman precedes the small grazing flock onto the dusty road leading to the stable and the house one way, and far away on the other. She gazes at the white walls in the shrinking light and, instead of going home, disappears into the distance along the path. She reaches the top of the hill, enveloped by the sunset, and starts walking down the slope on the opposite side. Her feet, knees, her swinging hips, her waist, her shoulders: she vanishes completely into the grass. Only a falcon remains, flying high.

I've dreamed my mother's end. A few images devoid of history, a grassy horizon that swallows her slowly. The place scared me. We never walk that way, it leads to abrupt gullies and to Saint Colomba's ravine, good for nothing but dying. The woman didn't look very much like her, but I'm certain I recognised her from the way she walked, the life that moved her. It's lost over time, in chunks, like her memory. She gives up living, she just is.

I dreamed of you last night. I came to look for you with Giovanni, but we couldn't see anyone, only the dusty road crossing the dull green field, a falcon flying above. Then you emerged from the other side of the hill, head first, then your shoulders, your waist, the swing of the hips, all of you. Like a sun rising, a dot becoming a whole circle of light above the line of the horizon. You were dressed in black, with a checked apron and rubber boots below. The sheep followed you, grazing all the way. Giovanni ran towards you, happy. When you came close, you had two small lambs in your arms, covered in white curls. You said: *they were born yesterday*.

Yes, it was you. Only a little younger.

You were coming back from Saint Colomba. Why did you go there? You know it's dangerous. Granny Serafina used to tell of animals and souls tumbling down that ravine.

The nightmare I turned into a dream for her has done her good. Her headache today came in violent gusts, she says. They'd pound on one spot, as if to obliterate it, then move to another, ceaselessly, with unchanged ferocity. Now the wind has retreated to the woods and you can barely hear it in the distance, a dull, muffled background. But until a little while ago the pain was biting like a wolf, and only just now have those fangs dropped their prey. She begs me to believe her. The old story-teller describes how the beast loped away, with his tail between his legs, turning once more to look back, ears pointing downwards.

It was something I told her that chased him away, but she can't remember what. I make a suggestion. She laughs at the idea of the lambs seeing off the wolf, the wind, her migraine. Agnus et lupus.

I help her look through the tin box where she keeps her crochet hook and balls of yarn. She used to crochet tablecloths, curtains, all sorts of doilies, she'd lose sleep over it, working to very complex diagrams in magazines. There's an exquisite white bedspread in the finest cotton yarn at the bottom of my wardrobe. I've never used it, I'm afraid to spoil it. I'll leave it to Giovanni, one day. It's made of seven hundred hexagonal pieces, each with a rose in relief, joined together and trimmed with a fringe. Clorinda, still a child, wanted to help at the start, but after a few trial hexagons she gave up: my mother's perfectionism found her sister's stitches too loose. She worked on it on her own for two years, spending every scrap of time on it when her hands would otherwise be idle: in the evening, in front of the fire, during the hours spent grazing the sheep, in her doctor's waiting room. I didn't care for that endless work. I never even thanked her.

She lifts the lid of the Danish biscuit tin, pulls out a long crochet chain, single, double and treble crochets alternating along it in no order. You can see from the knots where she got into difficulty, broke the yarn and started again. It's the web of a deranged spider.

Find me a pattern, she asks. We've already tried, even the simplest ones defeat her. The yarn becomes alien, hostile. It rebels, it teases, she can no longer master it. It compels her to do strange things, it's no longer safe.

I could sit next to her for a time and direct her, a double crochet, five chain stitches, three single crochets. With my head brushing against hers, I watch while the work grows in her hands, admire it. But I haven't yet decided to commit to her.

When she dies, I'll sink into the guilt I am accruing day by day. It'll be waiting for me at her funeral.

My guilt is an empty space, the vacuum left by my neglect. I neglect to give her love, I refuse her my hands. The care she most needs, I let her go without.

I dispense her own story to her, and a 10 mg memantine hydrochloride divisible tablet every twelve hours, in the mild hope that it will slow down the degeneration of her neurons.

Fioravante and Cesare were like two fighting cocks. Cohabitation ended one summer evening with a row over the timing of threshing. Cesare slammed his fist on the table, breaking both hand and wood. We moved in with the other father, a hard man, master of his family and of another piece of poor land, made up of steep slopes, some plots at quite a distance from the others. The most fertile, De Contra, was as far as the other side of the river.

It wasn't enough. You would sometimes rouse me from the thick sleep of dawn to wave Dad and the uncles goodbye. I'd stick my tousled head out of my refuge, the corner between the sink and the hearth, to peek at the suitcases by the door, your silent tears, your demure embrace. Only one mutual plea between you: take care, take care of the kid. I rubbed my eyes, brimming with unfinished sleep and the need to cry. I observed my grandfather's ancient profile, his jaw set. He seemed not to know emotion, and his children kept theirs hidden. It was necessary.

Our emigrants were seasonal workers: they'd come back before Christmas and leave again in February, for Germany or Switzerland. During the last few days of January the air at home grew thick with anxiety as we waited for the new contract, a yellow sheet of paper with German writing on it, of which we only understood the date, summoning the men back to the factory. Grandfather Rocco wasn't keen on European countries, he'd have chosen America, and always complained that there wasn't *a single 'merican in the family.*

In nearly all homes the young men, whether single or married with children, would emigrate. With the head of the family would remain only the firstborn son, who carried on working the land and looked after the children of the absent brothers. This was my father. But for a few years, while Grandfather could still manage with the help of the women, he'd go too. I hardly remember my dad as a factory worker, he rarely spoke of it. He said he lived with other Italians in wooden shacks near the factory, where they slept in bunk beds, many crammed in each room. He'd fix his work trousers with sticky tape that was also resistant to water, and would bring some back as an example of the proverbial Teutonic efficiency.

Look at the photos, they seemed in good spirits. There he's sitting on a mattress, wearing a vest, or busy giving a roommate a haircut, in this other one he's idiotically pointing at a half-naked woman in a magazine. And here? Visiting a concentration camp, with a friend from Calabria, maybe Dachau, he wasn't sure when he told us about it. Both dressed to the nines, with their moustaches duly trimmed, they had a photograph taken in front of the gates, next to the entrance to the crematory ovens. I don't detect a great deal of understanding on those faces.

This one here is Uncle Umberto, gardener in Switzerland. It's so funny: a land worker, used to growing plants to feed men and beasts, he gracefully moves among bushes and flowerbeds, busy pruning roses. Once, he was mowing the lawn of a block of flats when a violent sneeze made his dentures fly into a ground-floor open window. As there was nobody at home, he had to sneak in to recover his precious possession, shaking with fear at the thought of the inflexible Swiss police.

The excitement of return would hang in the air for weeks: you smiling constantly, the dogs on the alert, even Grandfather was less harsh. And there they were, one evening, exhausted after a journey by train, bus, shared taxis, the last stretch on foot. The suitcases, half-empty when they'd left, would come back full to bursting, precautionary string wrapped round them; I remember coats stiffened by the cold of a distant land, Terylene trousers with their approximate crease. Cesare smelled of cheap aftershave but above all he exuded the aroma, opulent and triumphant, of the fabled Swiss chocolate, even from his hair. Oh, the supreme sweetness of that day, once a year.

Kisses for the little ones, with the wives the same reserved demeanour of the day they'd left, and a manly composure with Grandfather. My cousin and I would fawn all over them with no restraint, until they'd pick us up in their arms. We'd smell the metallic stench of never-seen wagons.

After dinner we'd all sit around the fire, a little more talkative than usual, the light of the flames flickering on faces marked by an unfamiliar weariness. You would patiently unstitch the bundle from the internal lining of his jacket. It was the money to move out, to buy, one day, land of your own all in one piece, with no stones, no crevices, that you could work with a tractor, even irrigate, maybe.

All we children wanted by then was to open the suitcases and loot them of their treasures, to then fall into a heavy, dreamless sleep, with hot cheeks and open mouths smeared with chocolate.

Later, the grown-ups in bed too, conjugal intimacy would restore scents left behind, seasoned hay and winter stables, trapped in the women's hair.

At dawn they were already tending to the animals, observing them with the fair eye of one who's been away, pleased with the brooding beasts and their newborns. Once the light had grown brighter, they'd walk through the fields to assess the precision of furrows traced by others, the reassuring stillness of the land. Us children under their feet the whole time.

As children, we never understood why they had to go away. We knew nothing of money. Enclosed in our world, bounded by trees, clouds and solitude, we'd wake up early in the morning, drink milk from the cows on the lower floor, dunking bread made at home like the pasta we had for lunch and nearly everything else. Gifts would occasionally come from the outside world, dolls for me, the other toys made of earth, wood and imagination. Our fathers' every departure was a farewell, a bereavement, a betrayal of our hearts.

You all said it would be for less than one year. To us, newly arrived, the weights and measures of life meant little. To us it seemed forever.

We'll find them, don't worry. You must have lost them here, they're not small enough to vanish into thin air. I'm going to look everywhere, I promise. No, they're not in the fridge, I've opened it to get some water, I'm thirsty. In any case let's buy a spare pair. Everybody has two pairs, in case they lose them, or break them. It happens to me too, you know, not being able to find things at home. This summer it was a T-shirt I really liked.

Glasses equal to x equal to … no equation rescues me. I look for them through these rooms that resemble her mind. I've never been good at finding stuff, I'm not able to take things in like that. She misplaces objects more and more often. Last week it was the key to the cellar. We used to always keep it in the door, but then we had to put it away.

My father forced the lock, cursing half a calendar's worth of saints, and immediately found the key, shining on the brick floor.

Cesare is learning about patience. He adapts day after day to this woman, so different from the one who used to run our lives. He even shows tenderness, in that rough and clumsy way of his. He affectionately calls her simpleton and lazybones. He grabs the broom as if it were a spade and sweeps, carefully, always ready to hide the unmanly tool should he hear someone on the stairs. He tries to cook, experimenting and asking for advice. Above all, he copies what he has carelessly witnessed being done at the stove. He uses too much salt and overcooks, but he's not bad. When I tell him that, he shakes his head: it's necessary.

When I arrive after lunch, I find them sleeping on the sofa, one partly on top of the other, intertwined. It's not a true embrace but it recalls one; it's just what they can manage. In their sleep they're husband and wife, a life away from me. I watch them, the untamed septuagenarian and the sorrowful moon.

Occasionally he twitches, letting go of the screams inside. He opens up to a desperation he cannot name. I suppress my rage as he does his, I grind it up between my teeth. I tell him off, I keep telling him she doesn't do it on purpose, it's a sickness. As I utter the words I hope they'll persuade me. If she had cancer or diabetes we wouldn't be so unkind to her. We can't forgive her for having lost control of herself, of us.

Your aunt and mother-in-law, on the other hand, was sweet and maternal. I bear one of her two names, slightly altered.

Maria Concetta submitted to her husband's will with slight detachment, and was the only one he felt strangely intimidated by. She managed to soothe the air around her. She was openly an ally to her children, especially to the only girl, the youngest of four, and then to you, when we went to live there. After the troubled coexistence between Dad and Grandfather Fioravante, we enjoyed a bit of peace.

Grandmother didn't last long. She was operated on in the town of Teramo for a simple appendicitis, but she struggled to recover. Septicaemia, the doctors said. The ambulance took her to die in a hospital in Naples. Once there, you didn't leave her side for a moment during the last few days of her fever and agony. She called out for the children in her delirium. You gave the sheep's cheese you'd brought from home to an old woman visiting her sister at the same hospital. In exchange she prepared sandwiches for you, and comforted your pain and fear.

You sent a telegram to Cesare, in Germany. When he arrived his mother was still warm, a sheet over her face. He left again right after the funeral, money was needed to pay for Maria Concetta to return to Tossicia from Naples, and all the rest.

You became mother to Lucianella, only seven years younger than you. Before the bereavement I used to fall asleep in her arms at night, twirling my fingers in her tight curls, but never after; I could feel the loss on her body. My sticky hands began instead to pat her grieving cheeks with open palms, as if to caress or comfort, so my aunt says.

You often ask me, but I was too young to remember Granny. Barely two. One image lingers, only one, but it may not be her. A middle-aged woman sitting on a wicker chair, composed, with an intense and concentrated look on her face. She's wearing a grey cotton dress with small flowers. She looks towards me, or perhaps towards the lens of a photographer who is shooting her portrait. As they used to, then. You told me I used to love running to the Sestili photographic studio when we went down to Montorio. One day you refused to let me, because you didn't have enough money and I wasn't dressed very well. I screamed so much down the streets of the village that you felt embarrassed and gave in. You asked to be allowed to pay when you came to collect the print, and here I am, with my mud-splattered shoes, my trousers crumpled and my eyes still bearing traces of my recent tears. Look, my eyelashes were still wet, it looks like mascara.

So then, who were we talking about? About Granny... not Serafina this time, Maria Concetta. No, I was too young to remember her. A presence comes to mind, wearing grey with little flowers, I don't know if it is her. I don't look like her, so you've always told me. I only have one of her names, shortened.

No photographs were found. On her grave there is one cut out of a group photo from your wedding, but it shows her side, and her headscarf covers part of her face. You can only see her profile, she's looking at you next to her firstborn.

All his life he's called out to his lost mother in his sleep, sometimes it's a cry, a heartbreaking yearning. In summer he lies down on the floor of the balcony, it's cooler, he says.

When he turns on one side a sharp pain troubles him, he shouts oh mother.

Some years ago the tractor made a sudden start and the track crushed his right foot and ankle, his prompt reflexes barely saving his skin. We heard him scream. When we found him he was sitting on the ground, cradling his foot in his hands. He was drenched in sweat, a series of oh mothers alternating with the most ferocious profanities.

Only his mother responds to his pain with silence.

My parents have always loved each other. She has three small photos of him in her purse.

I felt marginal to their bond as a couple; the complicity between them would ignite a childish jealousy. I heard them sometimes, when I slept in their bed. The shaking of the bed would wake me, the animal energy next to my body. She was always at the bottom, passive, she seemed to endure it. He had the wild power of a randy bull.

From time to time I'd go with him when he took the cow in heat to be mounted by the only breeding bull in the Tossicia area. Cesare would pull her with a rope and I'd prod her with a light stick to push her in the right direction. She was very agitated, frothing a little at the mouth.

When we got there Dad would instruct me to wait outside while he went inside the stable with the bull's owner. I stayed in the yard, daydreaming. I imagined the bull, all black, as big as an elephant, his hair sleek with sweat, mounting my poor cow. She'd come out tired, calmer, saliva trickling from her muzzle. She was very different, something had happened to her.

My father replicated next to me the same power of that animal. Eyes closed, I'd pray that it'd be over soon, as you do during an earthquake. I'd hold my breath and then start again as evenly as I could, certain that he'd kill me the moment he caught me awake.

I don't think she ever enjoyed it. She must've accepted it as a necessary release. They loved each other anyway. Now she's much more dependent, she phones him all the time when she's home alone. She can still manage that, copying the number from the label stuck to the wall. Some days she even remembers it.

It's early on Sunday morning. From a distance the garden floats in a luminous mist; by the time I get there I can't make it out any more, the whole house is enveloped in it now. Over the Sleeping Giant range, scraps of clouds coloured by the vapour of the recent dawn linger. The memory of a plane draws a pink smoke trail.

There's a smell of damp here, of cracked earth and leaves. The plants are scorched to about halfway, higher up they're still green. They haven't been watered all summer. The tomatoes are at the top, small, attacked by green shield bugs. They start to rot from the side opposite the stalk, the brown stain widening and burrowing inside. I pull a ripe one, clean it on my sleeve and bite into it. It's slightly acid, and sweet, it tastes of the summer sun and of these first dew-wet nights.

These are the last ones, the most succulent. I find a small mound of them on the ground, my mother must have picked them yesterday and then forgotten them. I select a few, take off my cardigan and heap them in, tying off the sleeves.

Some of the melons are cracked and rotting, nobody picked them. They will mulch the ground for the next season. The ones born late won't ripen, they'll remain dark, useless little balls. The salad greens we haven't used have gone to seed, they're not good to eat any more. It's a time of disarray, the summer vegetables have completed their cycle. They lose their fullness, the leaves wilt and surrender to gravity. They die a silent vegetable death.

One day soon my father will sort it all out. He'll scythe the plants down to the ground and make a pile of them. He'll have trouble making the fire take, then be assailed by a thick and cloudy smoke. Later, he'll turn over the soil to expose the part that has rested, and leave it until the next sowing, in spring.

In the meantime he has prepared the winter garden, with straight, parallel furrows and seedlings of salad greens, fennel, Savoy cabbage and cauliflower. It's turned into a clear day now. Flocks of birds organise migrations in the intense sky. My mother calls me from the balcony, surprised. She's forgotten I've already been indoors to see her. What're you doing there? I'll come too.

I prepare myself to be invaded.

I suggest a walk along a neighbouring street. She talks non-stop, as usual, with short pauses when searching for a topic or waiting for a reply. She's itching to be cross at someone, settles on Uncle Remo. A topic she returns to at almost regular intervals. She tells of his suspicious looks, the ill-mannered tone he reserves for her, how cleverly he shuns toiling on the land, even his own.

She seeks my complicity, but finds me reluctant. He's my broken father, the distant emigrant drowning in alcohol the pain of seeing his son brought up by Cesare, the older, cleverer brother who got to stay at home to manage the family land. He was not the cheerful gardener strolling among Swiss bushes, he was the gloomy factory worker, the one we have no photographs of.

It upset me, the lucky one, that one father was with us but not the other, and I never resented Fabrizio, my one imperfect brother, being occasionally indulged. We owed him that.

I can't rant about my uncle. She's disappointed. She tries again and again, I change the subject. I ask her if she's given some of the tomatoes to Grazietta, whose garden was already scorched by August. When we come to the row of mulberry bushes bordering the neighbouring plot, she asks: won't you tell me a story today?

I'll tell you about the reddish satchel and the page of the book you showed me the morning of my first day at school. There were two pictures on the page, and below them some writing in block letters. Here it says mum, you said, and here, children. Then you walked with me to school, the first and last time.

I was worried while walking the two kilometres there. Wasn't I going to school to learn mum and children? Was I supposed to know it already? I followed you, articulating the words in a murmur, mum, children, trying to remember the corresponding marks, all those strokes and legs. I learned to read while walking, out of fear, from memory.

Some mornings I'd go a little out of my way to meet up with school friends coming from a different direction, but usually I'd walk through the wood. Still scared of wind and storms, I was happy when it was sunny. The path gently wended its way through oak and beech trees. The moss showed me where north was. I'd stop to pick primroses and cyclamens for my teacher, eat berries, and watch out for mushrooms, at a careful distance, to then report to Grandfather Rocco who'd come and pick them in the afternoon. My jaw dropped when a fox unexpectedly crossed my path. I saw it again on subsequent mornings, always at the same spot. It jumped in front of me and then walked away, turning back when it was at a safe distance. We'd look at each other, alone there in the wood.

Our teachers lived a long way away, so they never arrived before nine. We would light the clay stove and class would start. There were mixed-age classes. I was the only one my age when I got to year four, and Elsa, my teacher, got me to work all year with the fifth-year pupils.

I liked reading. You'd buy me children's books in Montorio, when you could, in secret. Thank you. And Imelda, who had a shop in Tossicia, from time to time would send me improbable volumes for a child, recovered from the dusty store where she kept the most varied goods. After lunch, in the half-light of my corner between the sink and the hearth, I'd leaf through the pages, breathe in the smell of ink, stroking gently with my fingertips the grain of the paper, sometimes cutting myself on the edges if the book was new. I looked forward to Imelda's books, passed through I don't know how many hands, the paper yellowed by time and the traces of unknown previous readers, a coffee stain here, a pencil mark or folded corner there. I delighted in them, through my hands and sense of smell. The subject of the book was less important than its smell.

There were a few houses by the school, in the largest of which lived Milva, a dark-haired little girl, beautiful apart from the shadow of a moustache on her upper lip. They had a television and access to a public phone, and she would eat oranges right under our astounded eyes, letting the juice trickle down her wrists. Open-mouthed, I'd count the drops falling in the dust. When I came home, still without electricity, I would find my little cousin Fabrizio sitting on the stairs savouring a banana, a gift from his maternal grandmother in Colledara. It's just for you, he'd been told, the other one is for tomorrow, I've left it on your mum's chest of drawers, so nobody will take it. I was nobody. A horrid person, you're right. Milva wasn't, though; a couple of times she gave me a segment to try. She married an artisan in Castiglione, Messer Raimondo, with a healthy bank account, but so tight-fisted as to force her into a life of hardship. You want to know where she is? She died of cancer last year, all that vitamin C didn't do much for her. You'd forgotten, better that way.

We get home and sit on the step to divide the tomatoes. She's happy. A gust of wind drops a yellow leaf in her lap, she chases it away instinctively. She also pushes away the cat, who has come to rub himself against our legs. I look at her in the October light; I am tempted into affection. She's an apple cast out some time ago to dry in the sun. We go upstairs. I feel uncomfortable. I know I must open the fridge door, I hold my breath. I turn round quickly, in three steps I'm there and I open it wide. It's half-empty. There is no mint-flavoured tripe, with bits of ham patiently scraped from around the bone. Nor the oven tray with the *mazzarelle* ready to go in the oven for Easter lunch. My mother used to prepare the strips of lamb's liver in advance, with marjoram and fresh garlic, then wrap them in endive leaves and tie the bundle with a clean strip of gut.

Now, on the central shelf, a paper bag doesn't promise anything good. I open it carefully, push my fingers in. She looks on dejected as I discover the broken glass inside. I pull my hand back, I didn't cut myself. I feel like crying and hugging her, but it's only an instant. I fold the paper again, put everything in a plastic bag and throw the lot in the bin.

Saint Imier 4 November 1970

Dear wife

I write this letter to let you know I am well and I hope you are too

Here it snows every single day when I go out in the morning to walk to the factory my nose hurts from the cold and tears fall on the front of my coat and they freeze right away

Hows Fabrizio is he growing? If he needs them make sure he gets some slaps Cesare won't lay a single finger on him because I'm not there but remember were not raising a little prince

Sometime arrange with Esperina to wring a chicken's neck behind fathers back he'd only kill the one at Easter and Christmas but little ones need more meat than we do

If you want to give the old man some meat too just tell him it was the dog that killed the chicken at most it will get a bit of a clobbering

Here in the shack we are all Italian and I get on very well with the others especially the Calabrians who are as stubborn as us from Abruzzi and on Saturday night we go to the bar to have a beer together

The boss treats us well and comes to the factory once a day he walks right by us to see how we work and nods his head yes

But the foreman is from Frankfurt bit shirty he don't speak French very well and when hes cross he shouts to us in German dirty Italian and Italian pigs spitting all over the place

*I never even look at him that redheaded prig and I take no
notice, I just carry on with my work I know I can do it*

*In October I did a lot of overtime and there was 100 francs
more in my envelope than before now I want to do it all the time*

*Friday my bottom wisdom tooth hurt and I howled all night
like a dog*

*On Saturday morning a friend took me to a female dentist he
knows and the tooth wouldn't go numb because it was inflame
so she punched me in the face to stop me screaming and just
wrenched it out that devil*

*Here women do what they like smoke cigarettes in the street
drink beer and answer back to men they even wear trousers*

*So it's better if you don't come over, even if we'd said you might
come next year and get in to do the cleaning at the hospital
where I know someone who could put in a word*

*Let me know if Esperina bosses you about I'll talk to her when
I come back and put her in her place at least its not long now
just over a month*

*Have Quaiarella and Camisciòla calved out yet? Have
they had males or females? Have you sown the wheat in De
Contra? And the barley?*

*Put a piece of loin aside for me before its all used up but hide it
well or there'll be none left like last year damn it*

*Its late now and I'm sleepy but I'll write another letter before I
get back*

*Give our Fabrizio lots and lots of kisses and Tina also and
greetings to everyone*

*A big hug to you too my dear wife from me your husband
Remo bye bye*

I'd never seen her so agitated. I was watching Aunt Lucianella from behind, she was busy washing up. The window over the stone sink framed the beech wood surrounding the Cirisciola fountain. Nothing could be seen because it was already dark, but she wouldn't stop looking that way. She dropped dishes, she twitched, she strained now and then as if listening to the mournful call of night birds.

She broke a glass. Grandfather Rocco swore to the Holy Face of Manoppello and threatened her. Bending over to pick up the shards with her still-wet hands, Aunt cut herself without uttering a sound, only I noticed that she was wrapping her finger in the dish cloth to staunch the bleeding. She mumbled she was going downstairs to dispose of the pieces out of my reach. Nobody answered.

She didn't come back. After half an hour, her brother Remo wondered aloud where the hell did she go. Grandfather sent him out to look for her. He looked in the stables, store rooms, all the nooks and crannies and came back with a long face.

At once you all realised what had happened. Her fiancé, Marcello, one of Fioravante's nephews, hadn't come to see her for a few evenings. It had saddened me because he always had a few sweets in his pockets. She'd faked a bout of flu, they'd been planning to elope. Grandfather started to shout, Dad went white and you burst into tears. But Uncle Remo really was fearsome. He ran out of the room like a crazy person and we heard him ransack the wardrobe and throw everything to the ground. He came back holding a gun. We froze. He calmly explained that he'd got it in Switzerland and then scrambled out into the night, the longest in my whole life. He didn't find them, of course. He returned at dawn blind drunk, without his sister, without his gun. He'd thrown it into the marsh.

It took a year of patient diplomatic work for relatives to bring about the reconciliation of the two families. She came one afternoon, when Grandfather and Remo were tending to the sheep downstairs. They'd been talking about the girl and crying, those fake hearts of stone. She arrived quietly just in time to hear a gruff intention of forgiveness, then one of them saw her and passed her the milk pail, just like before.

They were married in May, I wore a flowery dress and recited a sort of poem wishing them well. They gave me a banknote.

Afterwards I always wanted to visit and would stay for a few days, with the excuse that it was four kilometres away. I really missed her.

It was fun, at Lucianella's. The in-laws lived with the newlyweds in a yellow-painted house. Palmira, though, enjoyed pulling my milk teeth and, as soon as one started to wobble, she'd make me sit still and then pulled the tooth out with her own hands.

Once, I ran away to them.

The sheep mocked me at first when I went with them to the pasture, I didn't know how to guide them. I approached them too directly when they deviated from the path and – the stinkers – instead of retreating they'd go even deeper into forbidden land. That day I had to return them to the sheep pen through a path that cut through the fields of a rather crabby neighbour. They stopped to graze on new clover, I pushed them here and there without managing to get them back on the path. Frantic, I then saw you from afar, she's coming to save me, I thought. Instead you were livid because I was late and you cuffed the back of my head. I screamed from the pain and heartache and ran away through dog rose bushes until my heart nearly exploded in my chest, tears flying in the wind. When I reached my aunt, she comforted me. You arrived later, calmer, and said let's go home.

I stopped visiting when they served a roasted cat for dinner, passing it off as rabbit. I'd seen the oven tin with the perfectly roasted animal, the meat slightly reddish. I didn't recognise it, because they'd cut its head off. I ate my dinner and potatoes, then they told me the truth, all but Lucianella laughing like crazy. How disgusting! I used to play with that poor beast. I threw up out of the window and nobody ever let me forget it, because of the stains on the yellow wall.

The Christian Democrat mayor of Tossicia chose the Abruzzi minister Lorenzo Natali as godfather to his third born. This was the opportunity for him to visit his most remote district, ours. In two days we organised a festive welcome. It was Easter, but it snowed. The banquet had to take place under cover, at Milva's house, the one with the oranges and the television. Everybody contributed, everybody came with overflowing baskets balanced on mules, as we did on market day. A requisitioned cauldron bubbled away on the hearth of the first-floor kitchen, while mutton and chicken cooked in the wood oven. After the pie some photographs were taken, with the peasants standing all around the minister they'd voted for so enthusiastically at the previous election. The mayor explained that they now were at the end of everything: the road, electricity and water network all stopped there. He called me over and I told the Right Honourable about doing my homework on winter afternoons, by the light of an acetylene lamp.

A few months later, a bulldozer turned up at the border of the hamlet. I would run with my little cousin to watch it from a safe distance. We were entranced by the movement of the blade, I liked it even more when it shook its load off. I sniffed the smell of turned-over earth mingling with exhaust fumes. In the afternoon, when Tullio the operator jumped off and left in his green Simca, we would inspect the section he had excavated that day, beating the ground under our feet, panf panf panf.

I could not believe we were walking on a two-kilometre road that they were building just for us. I inspected the decapitated earthworms, the collapsed mouse dens, the bared roots.

When the bulldozer reached Macchia del Sorbo we could see it from the yard. Come on, we're up here, come and conquer us, we surrender! Then it dived into the woods and came out many weeks later, so close all of a sudden. Only Grandfather Rocco and the patriarchs of the other five local families were diffident, edgy. At lunch time it was no longer necessary for Tullio to eat overdone pasta out of his Thermos flask: he was now invited in turn to our houses, and at around four in the afternoon you or one of the others would take him a coffee or a glass of wine. At last came the lorries laden with gravel, it was laid out and the work was done.

Dad bought a white Fiat 850 from the Taraschi dealership in Teramo, registration number TE 50645.

A year after that, we had electricity. We bought a fridge and a television, it's either me or that box, said Granddad. They both remained and he became fanatical about the weather forecasts. Turn it up, turn it up, he demanded when he heard the tune. He'd plant his chair and himself one metre away from the screen and hell would break loose if anyone so much as squeaked. Leaning forward, his mouth slightly open, he would raptly take in Colonel Bernacca's words, his lips soundlessly moving as if repeating something obscure. When the Colonel signed off at the end he'd reprimand him for any mistakes made the night before, but would nevertheless wish him goodnight and then turn the television off to return to his spot by the fire. I would then turn the television back on. I was never able to persuade him that a storm was not the same as being windy. Tell that to Bernacca, cleverclogs, he's the one to talk about rainstorms and then it's windy.

Yes, of course I remember: before we got our television we'd watch the Sanremo song festival at Milva's, you, me and a few neighbours. Cesare didn't like it. I could then play with my fortune-blessed friend for a long time, and envy her to my heart's content. The festival distracted us only a little.

We'd walk home late, disturbing the sleep of the wood with our chatter and the songs we'd just heard. You were happy.

We never had running water in that house. The families would take it in turns to attach a rubber tube to the communal fountain to fill large saucepans for the kitchen and water the animals in the stables on the ground floor below. We'd wash in bits, with water heated in basins, little ones getting a proper bath in the tin tub.

We weren't that clean, to be honest. Us children would often have layers of *cuzzella* on our necks and knees, a dirt made of dead skin cells, grease, sweat and dust. It wouldn't come off easily. Not for me, because you'd scrub me hard enough to take my skin off.

At times we'd smell like umbrellas do when you don't open them out to dry.

In winter we would poo in the stables and our rustic etiquette required us to cover it with straw, perhaps out of respect for the cows. You're right, with animals, herbivores especially, it's not as disgusting as that of humans. When it was warm we'd fertilise the fields with it, there were soft and downy leaves to wipe ourselves with. In springtime, if you came across a poo with lots of fruit stones in it, you knew it was Granddad's, who loved cherries so much he'd eat them whole, just pulling the stalk off.

She laughs in dialect at our dirty memories. When I offer them to her she hangs on to them for a few moments, or perhaps a little longer, if they find deeper tracks.

Her memory is now a manuscript traced with invisible ink; I leaf through it page by page and hold it to the flame to reveal its secret.

My mother sometimes doesn't want me to do that. Then I look at the sheets from the outside, locked as they are in the mystery of their unavailability. Hidden within are topics of neutral appearance, that the illness chooses to protect by turning them into something unspeakable. It's not a coincidence. If I get close to certain knots she gets scared, she fends me off right away saying I can't remember, and refuses my help.

This didn't use to happen when I told her a story heard from her or others. It happens now, when I tell her about our shared past, the story in which I was born and then grew old enough to remember for myself. I know it from the inside, her part as well as mine.

Grazietta stopped me with a nod as I walked past her house, just now. Your mother brought me tomatoes in the summer because my garden was dry. While talking, she disappeared into the shade of the kitchen on the ground floor and I heard her bustle about for a few minutes. Say hello to her for me, she entreated me, putting a bowl of sheep's milk ricotta in my hands, still warm.

Look, fresh milk in lumps. We can use some of it as it is, and with the rest we can make a soft pudding. It was the only sort we had, apart from zabaglione, before we left the mountains. I haven't eaten it in years, neither have you, I bet. I'd forgotten all about it.

All we've got to do is sprinkle the ricotta with sugar and ground coffee and mix the black with the white. It smells divine. Let's put it in the ceramic bowls from Castelli, those with the cockerel pattern, they're in the cupboard above your head. We'll leave it in the fridge to rest, to let the flavour develop. Then we can decorate it with coffee beans, before serving. Giovanni and Pietro will come round later, a different snack for them. No, a little coffee powder will do him no harm.

Oh and Aunt Clo sends her regards, I bumped into her by the studio. She asked me how you are. Ah, she never comes to see you, the renegade? She phones you all the time, though. And she looks after her grandchildren when her daughter-in-law is at work. You're right, you've helped everyone and now you're the one in need they don't remember. In any case, Aunt said that she'll drop by with the children one of these days.

A month ago. The neurologist showed me the cerebral atrophy on the MRI scan, tracing the advancing nothingness with her index finger. Ah, you can see it now, I said, it didn't come up on the CAT scan three years ago. It could've been depression, three years ago.

After the parting pleasantries, I found myself walking lightly to the exit. So it wasn't I, who made her ill. I'm not that powerful.

My father wanted to know what cerebral atrophy means. I explained: the brain's drying out, it's shrinking. A shiver crept up my spine, as if the words hanging in the still air of the kitchen had been uttered by someone else.

I'm afraid of her. Of meeting her inside the bewitched mirror. Of her drawing me in with her hooked fingers. She hugs me so tight, as she's never done before. Behind her I catch glimpses of Granny, Great-granny, demented old women. They call out to me with the voices of spine-chilling sirens.

She's afraid. She's lost. Time's also lost. She doesn't know what day it is, what month, what year. She can't tell the seasons apart any more, can't tell it's autumn by looking at the garden, at the goose bumps on her still-bare forearms. She gropes her way through this dense fog.

Occasionally she finds me, and the dismay she reads in my eyes multiplies hers.

We never talk about our fears. We continue to pass them to each other in a yet-unfinished game.

I watch her in the soft light of the afternoon, under an after-the-rain-coloured sky. We go and look for eggs in the usual places. She talks to me about the chickens.

She fears us, always ready to find her out, to catch her making a mistake, even if only with a glance or our surprise. She's dependent on those who judge her, and how she must hate them, so tense, concerned, and if today's been a good day we're reluctant to accept it, we need to plan for the disaster that tomorrow is sure to be. Pessimists, she used to say of me and my father, shaking her head. The illusion that she's well, even if only for a day, frightens us. We're sick, along with her.

A big Christmas tree with the lights going out, one after the other. They fade silently until they vanish, or else they burst. Their splendour no longer outlines its shape, many branches are already in darkness. Every Christmas the lights are more distant from one another, more lonely. One night, only one will remain. I see myself there, waiting until the last one goes out.

My tree's still all lit up. The family defect is not showing yet, or perhaps the effects are still imperceptible. Perhaps the odd light has gone out, but it's not noticeable in the overall brightness. The circuits work well, the failing of one small dot doesn't compromise efficiency.

Her network has already exhausted all resources, the failing of a single synapse is all it takes for a residual ability to die out. It's a desperate system, but wide stretches of awareness still remain.

I assist, in my helplessness. I visualise what awaits her and tremble for myself. It's always like that, in the end. I build up my defences, I exercise my mind.

I challenge myself to remember the history lesson Giovanni was studying yesterday, while looking for the construction file for Atri Council town planning department. Darius dies in 486 BC. His son Xerxes once again attempts to conquer Greece. I can't find the file, where have I put it? The city states reach an alliance agreement. The Persian army marches towards Athens. There it is, the trainee's left everything ready for me on the other table. After a few days of fierce fighting at the pass of Thermopylae, the Spartan King Leonidas and his three hundred men are crushed by the sheer number of the enemy forces. I lock the studio, the handbag strap slides down my arm and I drop the file.

Next page as I walk down the stairs: Greek triremes were forty metres long and five wide, they had three rows of two hundred rowers and could reach a speed of twelve knots per hour.

History's not enough today. I'm scared. I need a simpler, more mechanical exercise.

At home, before going to sleep, I throw myself at the supermarket receipt like a bulimic on the last crumb of food in the cupboard.

I read it four times, fold it in two, and recite:

tuna steaks	€ 5.79
button mushrooms	€ 1.33
kitchen foil	€ 0.99
apricot juice	€ 0.65
TOTAL	€ 8.76

Thank you, see you again soon.

In the well-lit living room the aunts, settled in old armchairs, are gossiping about someone. The aroma of coffee and freshly peeled mandarins lingers in the air. I stand by the chimney, listening, my elbow resting on the mantelpiece.

The door opens silently. She bursts into the room and falls at my feet, hugging my legs. She's dishevelled, in disarray, on her feet a pair of cream-coloured moccasins I didn't buy for her. As I stand there, still motionless in amazement, a puddle of pee spreads under her, speckled with greasy yellow stains. I hook my arms under her armpits, trying to lift her. She resists me, in vain I ask my aunts to help me, they've disappeared. I manage to drag her to the bathroom, she gets into the bath with difficulty, I remove her clothes and start to gently wash my mother's body.

She's run away from the nursing home where we left her. Immersed up to her breasts, she is now unnaturally calm. She stares at a small damp stain on the wall in front of her. She opens her mouth, I'm hungry, I'm thirsty, she repeats several times. Drops fall into the water and I look up, only then understanding that they're coming from my face. She's very biddable, she lets me stand her up so I can rinse her, she obeys my hand coaxing her to turn. I admire her back; the white skin on her buttocks, still smooth and firm. She looks like me from behind, the swimsuit tan line surprises me, she's never worn one. I yank her round. She's me. The phone rings.

I answer it, my heart in my mouth. It's me. No, my mother. I rub my moist eyes. In a few instants I sort through my confusion. I fell asleep doing the exercise with the receipt, there it is on the floor by the bed. I was dreaming but the phone rang for real. It's early Sunday morning, I tell Esperina when she asks me if everything's okay at the studio. She's not aware she dialled my home number; like every Sunday she's surprised not to find me at work. Come over then, she lures me. Yes, later.

The nightmare is a slimy web, sticking to my skin, to my spirit, as I wake. I can't forgive myself for shutting her out, for forcing her to break out and search for me, in her condition. Her hugging my legs stings more than being struck with a whip. I can't bear to have her on her knees in front of me, begging. I don't want to be the one in the bath.

I'm surprised to find her so calm. She's alone, my father is out hunting. She lit the fire herself. Out of place only her summer slippers. We sit by the fireplace. Tell me more, she says.

They brought us light and a road. We found our way and left. It was Cesare's dream: a farm with gentle slopes, spring water to train, a vineyard, a few olive trees. With money sent by the uncles from abroad, some savings and a sizeable debt you bought an old farmhouse at auction, in the Atri district, and sixteen hectares of longed-for land around it.

Along its boundary ran the provincial road, with bus stops to take children to school in the village and the women to market on Mondays. My father could finally get a tractor and use it without risking his skin in an overturn on a scarp. He wanted nothing more: to be part of a world we'd only ever seen from afar.

The same mountains along the horizon, with the profile of the Sleeping Giant, or, depending on who you spoke to, Sleeping Beauty, with its long rocky mane dipping towards Ascoli. We were a little further away now, better to see the sun set in the distance, instead of it going down over our heads.

It wasn't an easy move. We were not moving from one apartment to another. There were animals, farm tools, growing crops, and me having to change school. For one year you went up and down between Tossicia and Atri, where I attended the fifth year of primary school, staying with Aunt Clo, who lived in the historic centre with her two children, her husband who worked as a carpenter and her invalid father-in-law. I stayed with her for convenience, while we settled in the new place.

Uncle was kind towards me, we used to play cards together. But some evenings I would hear them arguing in their room, or rather he would argue and his wife: shh, shh. Then blows and her muffled cries. She begged him to stop. In the next room, which I shared with my cousins, I'd sit up in bed, gasping for breath. One night my aunt came in, her face crumpled, her tears hurriedly wiped away. Little Stefania was crying because the noise had woken her up. Barely containing her sobs, her mother pretended it had been the wind against the windows. She had her back to me and behaved as if I were asleep. The following morning, a bruise on her cheekbone and more on her arms, I caught a glimpse of her coming out of the bathroom. She immediately covered herself with a long-sleeved top, superfluous in the heat of those days.

But the rotten soul in that house was the paralytic old man who, hawking and spitting all day, goaded his son to clobber that useless female. Every day he'd think up reasons to recommend a good beating, if he'd been strong enough he'd have done it himself, never mind that pushover, as he called him. He never used her name, a sort of grunt was enough to call her over, and to others he'd always say your wife, or your mother, or your aunt. I wished him a slow and painful death, but instead the God he called as witness to his martyrdom took him peacefully in his sleep, after many years, allowing him plenty of time to blight the life of the one who looked after him. I never told anyone of the hell my aunt lived in. I was complicit in her silence, even as I knew that it deserved to be broken. I was afraid, her fear was infectious.

The first day at school in Atri no teacher would have me, because I came from a mixed-level class from the mountains. The headmaster eventually suggested to my mortified aunt, who had come with me, that she do the rounds again with my report card, and finally Miss Vanna took me in out of pity.

She died a few months ago, there was a bad grammar mistake on the death announcement posters. I saw her escape the cemetery one night, running through the village streets in her light-coloured boots, to correct the mistakes with her blue and red pencils. She would stop at each poster, *zac zac zac*, three bold marks, serious mistake. I dream a lot, yes. I can't remember last night's, though.

The animals were the last to leave. It was a permanent migration. You left at dawn, after a last feed in the stables you would leave behind.

You drove the animals with the help of a few neighbours and dogs, cows in front with the calves following, and about a hundred metres behind, the small woolly flock and the three goats. For a few kilometres it was old cattle tracks or grassy paths, then also sections of tarmacked provincial road, where the sheep left a trail of small black droppings and were overtaken by cars driving at foot-pace. From time to time a shower would fall on the migrating company and hooves would sink deeper into the rain-sodden ground.

It was late afternoon by the time you arrived, our new neighbours welcomed you and helped you sort out the animals. They'd brought bales of good hay. The cows were agitated, they shook their heads and bellowed, sniffing and pulling back from the water for a long time before drinking it. They were bubbling at the nostrils.

For a few years still you'd still take them to the mountains in summer; after that, a life sentence in the stable. The milk never tasted the same again, there were no more flowers.

The chickens travelled in threes or fours in the boot of the Fiat 850, their legs tied together. It stunk to high heaven afterwards, and there were feathers flying everywhere.

The new environment didn't suit the goats, they missed the broken ground, the wild country, the thorns. There was less milk, they were sad. Goats don't bleat, they sing, and they weren't singing any longer. Dad practically gave them away to a neighbour in Tossicia, the same who now uses our never-sold land for grazing.

I went back home last spring, with Giovanni. I didn't tell anyone, I thought it would have been painful for you to come along. You have to walk from my old school; the road the minister wanted for us is choked with weeds and undergrowth. We walked along the path I used to take after my lessons. Giovanni hadn't realised I had to walk so far every day. I showed him the spot where a grass snake brushed against my ankle, where I used to find strawberries, the hollowed ancient oak where I used to hide my little treasures. I have seen the metallic green flight of the scarab beetle over flowering elder.

We walked through the now untended field where Gennaro, our neighbour, mowed Bill's legs as well as the fodder grass. He had bought a BCS mower and was so proud of it. Our dog bounced barking around him, excited by the novelty, unaware of the danger. Gennaro, not yet familiar with the tool, wasn't able to stop in time.

Bill was Cesare's greatest friend in the animal world, the only pointer he'd ever had, with his red patches – all the other hunting dogs were setters. Bill was as meticulous in the hunt as he was playful when at home. He and Dad had an instant understanding; after the accident they just looked at each other, the amputated beast and the helpless master. He asked another neighbour to put him out of his misery, because Gennaro was sobbing with his head in his hands and didn't want to do it. But Ostilio managed to miss the shot at one metre away. Cesare grabbed the quivering gun and fired with precision, then threw it into the grass. I told Giovanni that Bill's wounds were superficial and that he and Granddad hunted together for many years after.

We reached the houses. Collapsed roofs, brambles climbing over walls. Through the staircase a tree has grown, alien. I ventured up two or three steps. I stopped: too dangerous with the boy behind me. Shrubs everywhere in the large communal yard, and weeds of all sorts, a jungle, almost, a little sinister.

Who knows how far the seeds were blown before settling there, in our yard. After the dwellings were abandoned, nature reclaimed the unused spaces, it destroyed our work, threaded ivy through cracks, stretched undermining roots under the foundations. Houses need people if they are to last.

There is a silence there now, without us. Only gusts of wind, birds, insects buzzing. A branch snapping under the weight of the snow makes an eventful noise. Stones fall when water soaks into the dilapidated walls and then freezes and expands in the cracks. At a precise moment, the first tile came off the roof. After that, ruin came easy.

Once the last flakes had fallen, Dad would go out in a pair of totally inadequate boots and trace my route, treading down a path of hardened snow so that I could get to school without sinking into the whiteness, without getting my feet wet. Then, at night, chilblains would plague him. I don't know why I think of that now, and tears come, it must be nostalgia. Dad treading down the snow for me. I never said thank you. There was no need.

Mum, you have a check-up today. You won't need to take your clothes off, just talk to the doctor for a while, that's all, she's so nice. You don't like her, she asks too many questions. Don't worry, it's not an exam, she won't get cross if you make a mistake. She only wants to know how your memory is, adjust the treatment. Why do you say her medicines are no more than sugar pills? It's not like you to be so pessimistic. Go on, it's only a test. The jacket's too light, I think, better take the woollen one and wrap up, it's cold. It'll take an hour to drive there, I'll tell you some more on the way.

The first few years it was hard. We had debts and bad luck. It rained indoors, into containers placed under the holes in the roof, and at every downpour Granddad would cuss, a soloist in a concert for drops and basins. But nobody was allowed to call it a storm, storms were made of wind. At the end, we would empty out the buckets of rain. When sparrows nested under the roof tiles, dust and fine soil would snow down on our intent faces, turned up at wooden beams alive with little legs and fluttering wings.

One Easter Friday, a little grey feather wafted weightlessly down onto Cesare's salt cod, and he said, enough. He made some calculations: he'd have to take on more debt, but he could count on the uncles' Swiss francs and the imminent sale of the calves.

As soon as the builders demolished the roof, the Flood started. You and Dad slept in the cellar, the rest of us with various neighbours. The old people confabulated, there'd never been such a wet spring, unless perhaps in '58, yes. The first floor was covered with large plastic sheets stretched between the outside walls.

It rained. Granddad fell silent. Walking through the tools the builders had left lying around, I stepped on a piece of wood with a long rusted nail sticking out of it. It went through my shoe and my foot. The next day it was swollen and infected.

One by one, the calves died of dysentery. You gave them injections as expensive as they were useless. They were reduced to skin and bone, trembling with fever, shit dripping down tails and hind legs already caked with it. Then they'd collapse to the floor, unable to get up again. They looked at us with their big eyes, waiting to die. Only two were left in the end, Cesare's favourite and another.

The favourite went in a sunset of pounding rain, Dad on his knees next to it. He cried, hands and chest turned to the sky, threatening the Almighty, hurling his disgust at him. Then he slammed his fists on the head of the creature, still warm from a life just departed. He sobbed, bent over the red coat of the newborn. His tear fell on its lifeless eye.

We listened close, you, my cousin and I, two steps behind him, mutely sharing his pain.

You too, you too. We'd never seen him cry.

The following morning the sun rose, after weeks, over our misfortune. The other calf recovered from the fever. You see, once in a while you have to show your rage. What do you mean, who to? To God. Father and daughter, sinners both? Maybe. But that time Cesare behaved better than God. All right all right, I won't say more, no blasphemies. Look, we're here.

It's dark by the time we leave. The unfamiliar smell of the sea reaches her in minute droplets, I ask her if she can feel it. She answers curtly and walks on, shut down and hostile. She needs to follow my legs, hers won't remember where we left the car, and she can't leave me behind as she'd like to. And yet the neurologist told her that she found her in good form. My mother doesn't care, she knows the result would've been very different if she'd taken the test an hour earlier or later.

These visits humiliate her. They poke around in the wound. She's made to face her illness, to account for it to someone else. I wait for her outside and when the door opens she recognises the look between me and the doctor, she senses the unvarnished truth behind the formal code of language. She's silent. Extrovert as she is, she will not speak of this. She will sometimes use clichés to refer to the ugliness of old age and her head like a sieve, or she might assert that she's been feeling better, these last few months. But her tone is light, almost flippant. She protects the hard nub of her pain.

I guide her arm in the right direction, try to imprint the slow rhythm of a stroll onto our steps. She doesn't tune in, I must slow her down, she's thrown forward off-balance towards an uncertain destination, urgent errands to take care of before it's too late. She can't walk without a purpose, but she's forgotten what it is. Where are we going, she asks. To eat fish in one of those restaurants glittering across the road, I'd like to say. Instead I look towards the indistinct mass of the Adriatic Sea, I breathe its smell deeply, and decide to save her the bother to justify her *no*. I'm taking you home, I reassure her. Her bad mood has melted away from her face, she waits expectantly for the story to start again. We've reached the car park, and I press the button to activate central unlocking. She tries to open the door of the car next to mine.

I tell her of when we cut the red plastic money box with the white stripes. It was so full it no longer jingled, it'd taken years to fill it. We made thousand-lira piles with ten, fifty and one-hundred lira coins, then wrapped them up in newspaper. They'd be used to buy sugar, coffee, exercise books, what was needed. I felt proud of my contribution to the family finances at that difficult time.

In the meantime the house had been made ready: functional, anonymous, the grey plaster on the outside left as it was. Gone were the old brick floors, the staircase parapet honeycombed by the brise-soleil, the tile roof with a thin layer of moss on the north side, and the nests of those poor sparrows underneath. The tiles remained piled at the foot of the elm tree, not yet affected by the disease that would kill it later. You preferred the new ceramic tiles to the terracotta ones, worn by generations of people; they were easier to clean. We wiped off a history that had barely been ours.

We were all happy. An indoor bathroom for the first time, with pink fixtures. And I finally got my first period.

Other calves were born, two cows had twins. The land was good. At dawn Granddad Rocco would sit on the veranda, gazing at the growing vineyard and the row of apple trees stretching towards the horizon. He'd roll a cigarette with shag tobacco and then smoke it silently, narrowing his eyes at every drag. Then he'd be off to work the land. He was fond of pigs. In September and October he patiently gathered fallen apples for them. They loved those; when they saw him walk up to the sty with a heavy bucket they'd be all over him, like dogs. The apples for ourselves we picked from the branches, to keep on a bed of straw in a little storeroom. Granddad called it the apple room, it smelled of apples even when they were gone. Never had as sweet an apple since. They lasted nearly all winter, because he rationed them a bit. Over the years they shrank in number and size, the trees were old, until Dad cut them down and replaced them with young saplings. He only left the one, for old times' sake; it gives apples the size of walnuts.

At four o'clock sharp on Thursday afternoons in summer, the mad ice-cream maker would come from Cellino Attanasio in his dark green Fiat Seicento Multipla. A few bends away from the house, the loudspeaker would be heard croaking a *pizzicarella* and we'd run, all the children in the neighbourhood, to wait for him on the road clutching our sweaty coins or, if we had none, a few eggs collected earlier.

He kept the ice-cream in a lidded wooden box wrapped in old tablecloths, to preserve it cold. He'd challenge himself to sell his handmade delight in improbable pastel colours within an hour, tops. We could choose between cone or cup and then he'd ask us to pick a flavour, for fun – they were all the same, the only difference between strawberry and pistachio being the colourant. I recall the taste of nothing, of spun ice, but we liked it. Even Granddad Rocco would have one occasionally; today I feel like having an ice, he'd say. Your father-in-law, no, he isn't with us any more. Remember that time we caught him tucking into a jar of Nutella? In spoonfuls, no less. And not a little coffee spoon, a tablespoon. He called it nutrella.

On Friday mornings it was the fishmonger's turn. Granddad would always go on about the money wasted on that food so alien he always refused to even taste it. But we managed to pass him off clams for mushrooms, and then it was plateful upon plateful of spaghetti. With tomato sauce, mind, or you couldn't have got away with it.

Here we are, we're back just in time to start cooking.

My father has prepared a fire for us. He's going round the stables now, to lock up for the night after a last check on the animals. My mother takes her jacket off, but finds it difficult to let go of her handbag, she holds it tight. I set the table. I help myself to salad before adding salt to theirs, I prefer mine without. While I grill sausages on the embers I hear her bustling around the table with the dishes, and I turn around. She has moved her plate next to mine; going back and forth she takes all my lettuce. Then she looks around, uncertain, she can't remember where she sits. She sets the plate on top of Cesare's and sits down. She doesn't wait for us. She chews slowly, her gaze fixed. She's so tired. Every now and then she asks won't you eat, or if I need help.

The three of us are at the table now. After the salad, she stares at the tablecloth, the glasses, lost. She bites into the bread. I serve her two sausages, and once finished she reaches with her fork to a spicy liver one, she doesn't recognise the colour. I warn her, she puts it down. After a moment she does it again, I repeat that it's hot and she leaves it. She picks it up again, Cesare says go on try it, she bites on it and complains, leaves it in front of him. He savours it, laughing, he'd even held back on the chilli, he says.

We push our chairs towards the hearth. My mother suddenly touches my leg and asks about my skirt, so soft. Is it new? Her misshapen fingers appraise the fabric, all the time with her hand on me. That's what she wants. She wants me. She does that often with my tops, she takes my arm and considers the workmanship. I could do that with my eyes closed, she says brazenly. She lingers on the wool, moves away, sliding her hand slowly from shoulder to wrist, like a caress, a wistfulness.

I can't stand her touching me, it troubles me. I'd like to be able to close my eyes tight and wait until she stops, trembling slightly. I repress my reaction. I try to come across as available but I don't believe I am, I'm rigid. Where her palm rests, my skin burns under the fabric. She's met with a piece of ice, dry and rough, a dusting of brine on the surface which attacks and burns. When she leaves me I'm irritated, for a while.

She still seeks me, only at times. She can't find me. She seeks me. As for me, I'm scared.

Now we're sitting next to each other in silence. She has withdrawn. I'm slipping inside her, I can feel it. I'm losing myself in the expanse of her emptiness. When I think I've gone mad enough I return to myself, to my familiar fear. The same telephone number, sometimes I remember it, sometimes I don't. A few days ago a friend said over dinner that his father had only one virtue, I can no longer remember which. That actor must have performed in another film, but I can't remember the title. Are these the failings of an overtired memory or my legacy catching up with me?

I envisage myself in twenty years' time, at more or less my mother's age. I am already wistful for what I will have forgotten. I long for the person I will have been.

She nods off, her head drooping. I push my chair closer to hers and offer her my left arm to rest on. She sidles closer, and immediately relaxes. I look at her sideways, I sniff her. She doesn't smell of anything, only of the heat of the fire that envelops her. I focus on the flame, calmly. Her body rests on me with a slight vibration, it pulsates gently, persistently.

My father lists small daily worries, he talks about her before she wakes up, before she can hear. He gets me up to date. He tells me that yesterday he found her pecking with a spoon from a saucepan containing the leftovers for the dogs: cold pasta, chunks of stale bread, gnawed bones.

We settle in a long silence, evading each other's gaze so as not to see our pain reflected in the other.

I'd never seen a more fearful tool than the iron circle Don Cesidio Sparacannone carried in the pocket of those trousers, held up by filthy braces. He'd sit at the table in the tenant's kitchen, legs wide open to make room for his big belly, straining fit to burst under his shirt buttons. Of an indefinable age over fifty, he was nearly bald, and the crown of surviving hair didn't quite reach over the folds of fat at the nape of his neck. In his mouth, the spaced-out upper teeth would intersect the ones alternately spaced on the lower jaw, in a crocodilian arrangement. Blobs of saliva foamed at the corners, stretching over between his lips like a yellowish elastic band when he got worked up in an argument.

Once he'd settled, your sister was to serve him a glass of house wine and place all the eggs on the plastic patterned tablecloth. The selection would begin. First, a long drink followed by a shiver of pleasure and a smack of the tongue. Then he'd focus his weeping piggy eyes on the ring, held in his left hand, while the sausage fingers of his right hand tried to get an egg to go through: if it did, the egg belonged to the farmer, if it remained set like a gemstone it was his, or rather, the landowner's.

Don Cesidio, lord to the servants and servant to the landlord, oppressed the tenant families who lived and worked on the various estates of the Cantalupos. Standing on one leg by the table, her arms folded, Diamante looked at him, surly, whispering to herself I hope you vomit blood.

Two communities of eggs formed on the table: on one side those that the hens had given without effort and on the other, the big ones, who had been birthed through pain.

Aunt would arrange the latter in a wicker basket padded with straw. Careful, if any broke later she'd be blamed for it. The provisions would then disappear into the boot of the Cinquecento Familiare, along with freshly picked vegetables, two plucked and gutted chickens, a five-litre jug of olive oil, three flasks of wine, jars of sausages and pickles, and a fresh or seasoned cheese round, depending on the time of year. Who knows if madam will be satisfied, the sleazy old man would wonder aloud, stinking up the yard with the fumes of his departing banger. The satisfaction of his mistress depended on the quantity of stuff he'd manage to pilfer before making his delivery to the Cantalupo mansion.

One winter evening Diamante asked your father for his permission to marry Gaetano, who'd been coming round to court her for some time. The patriarch, sitting half asleep by the fire, watched her through the customary half-open eye and then stood up, clearing his throat. The daughter of a communist may marry a sharecropping tenant, he pronounced, but she must know that it will not be easy.

After a few months Aunt left home with her man's ring on her finger. Shortly afterwards, her in-laws died and children came, one after the other. They lived inland in Atri, out of sight of the sea. We'd visit from Tossicia, Cesare would look around him and fall in love with the countryside, so like that of his dreams. It was his brother-in-law who let him know that the bordering property was for sale and encouraged him to take the first step. I'd like to buy it myself, Gaetano said, but I don't have two liras to rub together, Cantalupo and Don Cesidio have me by the throat.

So we became neighbours, and the year Aunt Clarice came to stay with us, the three of you were within earshot of each other. Diamante lived four or five hundred metres away, but when the tractors were turned off you'd call out, Diama' Diama', with your hands held like a loudspeaker to your mouth, and she'd answer, oooooh. In time her father's prophecy came true, with her working like a desperate, proud donkey staying on its feet through the sheer force of hatred. You helped, you'd always find a moment to run over with a bundle in your hands and a stream of kind chatter that would, sooner or later, trick a smile out of her.

The landlord wouldn't visit them often; he was a wiry man with a face pockmarked by the aftermath of youthful acne that no wealth had managed to heal over. He exerted a cold, hard power over his subordinates: Diamante was always fearful of him and, when Gaetano wasn't there, she'd call her children to her as soon as the white Mercedes entered the yard. She feared he'd bother her. Cantalupo was said to take tenants' wives in barns, behind sheaves of grain, in the stables, even. All exciting places for him, that mangy dog of a wife was enough for his bed. He never did try it on with Aunt, only once he stroked her cheek with the back of his index finger, while Gaetano was looking elsewhere. But little Eva, married to a tenant in the neighbouring district, gave birth to a child who was the spitting image of his father and master and, as a young man, had the same acne ravage his face.

The wife, you never saw her around, she governed from afar, giving orders to her husband, the husband to the steward and the steward to the tenant or his wife. Don Cesidio stole from tenants and owner alike, and was hated by all. Cantalupo stole the fruit of other people's labour, with the blessing of an unjust law on the division of produce between the parties.

Diamante took to stealing her own, blameless thief of creatures and fruits born into her calloused hands, the fingers chapped and blackened. She hid food for her family to live on, for her retarded son who'd spend all day on the stairs lost after the soaring flies and then, suddenly, a clapping of hands.

Mindful of her chicks, she protected them from the fox. A little duck found drenched and shivering in the grass after the rain, about ready to give up the ghost, would be kept by the fire in an old woollen sock, and fed a thin cornflour paste. She'd name it, Luigina, so she could call it gently back to life. She might find the bundle dead at dawn, but more often than not it would recover and return to the yard with its siblings. It was barely grown up when it caught Don Cesidio's eye: the one by the pigsty, pluck it for me tonight, Diama'. Aunt would secretly swap her for another, Luigina by now was her daughter and only old age would take her away.

Under a master she took to grumbling, more often than not against the steward. One of these days I'll tie you to that infested oak, and let you sweat all that fat under the scalding sun, or, if he carries on like this I'll shred the skin off his face, the old swine. It wasn't easy to fool him, he'd count heads of lettuce, garlic bulbs, onions, noting everything down on a little check notebook in dense, tiny handwriting. Tomatoes ripened in waves: at the first he'd estimate the entire crop for the season and convert it into bottles of sauce for delivery to the mistress. If then a hail storm or drought destroyed the rest, well, that wouldn't be anything to do with Don Cesidio or the Cantalupos. Take it up with the Almighty, how you must have cussed Him, Gaetano would get for an answer when he asked for the demand to be reduced.

Diamante would blame raiding foxes for the disappearance of chickens butchered at night to escape Sparacannone's unpredictable visits. He'd then ask the children what they'd had for lunch and would provoke them by accusing their mother of never putting meat on the table. Aah, Don Cesi', answered the eldest, she made an omelette with them little eggs you left us the other day. Then he'd unstrap from his shoulder a little shotgun made of reeds and point it at the fat chest, bang bang, I'll kill you a chicken if you want one. There was no fooling that boy.

The threshing machine was a sun-faded, red dinosaur, that swallowed sheaves on one side and, through a system of pulleys and rotating belts, spat grains from the other. You could unscrew the wooden components under the belly of the beast, and part of the grain would collect there unbeknown to the steward, who'd be all taken with counting the sacks filling at the outlet points. He wouldn't even wait for the machine to move away from the yard, so busy was he with removing grain to the landlord's stores, including the usual pit stop to lighten the load. Then the farmer could recover and sieve his secret harvest, future bread.

With Cesare's help, Gaetano would spirit away the embezzled four tons into our stores, to come back for it a little at a time, when there was need for it. As a proud smallholder, my father's blood would boil at the injustice suffered by his brother-in-law and, as a neighbour, he didn't lack the opportunity to pick a fight with Cantalupo or his messenger. The first came when the cost of bringing running water to us, newly arrived, and to Uncle, who had needed it for years, had to be divided. The first part is in common, we'll pay half each, Dad said, the rest is only for you. No, Don Cesidio insisted, all had to be split in half. Cesare asked him to be reasonable, attempting to control the rage rising in his chest. He started to draw the route of the pipes in the dust with a stick, stressing more than once that only one section would be shared. Uncle listened in silence, leaning his back against the door of his old Fiat Seicento. Ignorant peasant, the steward let slip. My father pointed the iron prongs of the pitchfork at his bellybutton, promising him that soon his guts would hang on the line like women's stockings. The coward took refuge in Gaetano's car, shrieking at him to start right away and later Uncle told us of the fireworks of farts he'd let off inside the narrow cabin. Such was the effect of fright on Don Cesidio Sparacannone.

As the years went by things improved a little for Diamante, as the percentage of crops was adjusted in favour of tenants, who'd been reduced to famine on lean years. Aunt remembered who her father was, and found out her rights. She straightened her back and stopped mumbling, she'd shout and threaten instead, if she had to. In 1982 Law 203 converted ancient agricultural covenants into rent agreements issued to independent small farmers, opening the way for many lawsuits between landowners and farmers supported by the trade unions. There had to be a Gaetano versus Cantalupo. It dragged on for years, and in the meantime Uncle was forced to rent from another landlord. Disappointed by the trade unions, he finally withdrew his demand for compensation. He managed to buy a scrap of land with a one-storey house on it shortly before getting sick with lung cancer. He had never smoked. He'd never breathed free air.

When I went to see him, a month before he died, he was spitting a foamy mucous into a plastic cup he held in his hand. I smelled his odour, like a wet hen. He was sitting in the kitchen and made an effort to speak. I couldn't bring myself to drink fruit juice out of a cup the same as his.

Diamante, standing behind him, ran her fingers through the few sweaty strands of hair. She looked at me, beyond words.

Addolorata was a brick outhouse of a woman, a professional recruiter of Abruzzi women as hired hands for large vine growers in the province of Verona. She'd come out of the dusty brown Fiat 129 that had just screeched to a halt in the yard; breathless and red in the face she'd ask, without so much as a good morning, if you'd to go with her to the vine harvest. As she spoke she'd wipe her forehead with a less-than-clean handkerchief. A good forewoman can scout the backstreets with her eyes closed; she knows where cash is needed to get the children back to school, what with new books and clothes fit for the coming season.

At the end of summer the harvest was done, the preserves already bottled and stored away in the cool of the larder; you could go and still be back in time for the sowing. So on occasions you experienced the emigrant's journey yourself: you filled a small bag with enough for a month and a half, and climbed into Addolorata's bus. I missed you, even though I was older by then and Aunt Clarice would often come by.

Standing on the grape cart, you'd cut off each bunch and let it fall into the enormous funnel held in your left hand. All day with your arms up in the air, the juice dripping down to your elbows, mingling with the dust and salt. Wasps buzzing around you. At night you'd wash and laugh with the others in the large farmhouse among the vineyards, incessant chatter from bed to bed until sleep got the better of you. That's the way of women. No, I wasn't there, but I've chatted the night away with student friends, that's how I know, and from the tales on your return. From Verona you'd bring me undershirts and anecdotes about Addolorata, who'd take her shoes off on the train and so found all the space she needed to sleep in comfort. Or the time they woke her at the Brenner Pass to ask for her passport and she answered passport my arse, I'm going to Verona.

She died one winter afternoon, as she played cards with a bunch of men in the bar on the square, in her village. She was gone already when the cigarette fell from her lips.

I would often fall in love, in my teenage years. I had to be in a feverish state, as soon as the temperature dropped I'd become infatuated with someone else. I got up to all sorts to meet my boyfriends, absence from school, pretend study afternoons with friends; I was good at making up excuses, especially with Dad, who was so strict. You were easier, but I fed you my lies anyway so as not to put you in an awkward situation with him. I was trouble, I know, but you never fell for any of it. You laugh, so it's true.

Giuliano was the most elusive of my loves, the only one to leave me. I wanted to poison myself because of him, did you know? You kept a large blue plastic tub in the cellar, for marinating olives. Kneeling next to it, my tears rained into the dark liquid in which caustic soda had been dissolved. I filled a ladle and took it to my barely open lips. I was shaking.

At that moment, the cat came and meowed at me. I burst out laughing, splashing the liquid all around. Ironic green eyes fixing his mistress intent on improbable suicide by brine, he meowed again, are you stupid, and then started triangulating the hams. I wasn't talking to the cat, he was the one talking.

You were always taken in. If I brought a boy home more than twice you'd fall head over heels for him and were so disappointed when it ended. You promised you'd send us both rolling down the stairs if I ever brought back anyone else. But you'd only fall for them again, after I had.

I wanted to be the opposite of the daughter you wanted, that's why I married Andrea. It's not so simple, it wasn't just that, but that too. I'm telling you now. I got married to spite you and separated for my own sake. And so I betrayed you twice. When I announced we were splitting up, you cried and Dad never said a word. He slept in the stable for a few nights, to let me and the world know how I had shamed him.

They knew I had to get free. They accepted it, painfully.

Under geometrically perfect eyebrows, Andrea's irises were so dark that the white around them appeared to be blue. He wooed me with his celestial gaze and the twelve-string guitar he played along to songs in made-up English, arranged on the go. He was different, a gypsy angel almost without a sense of duty, no sense of guilt, either.

He'd given up the post of non-specialist workman and was working for me, as a surveyor. In the meantime, the house grew, with me, the architect, always on the telephone, running to the building site, dealing with the builders. After it was finished, we'd have his parents, brothers, nieces and nephews round for Sunday lunch, dinner too. I cooked for everyone. Him, smoking, on the black leather chaise-longue, listening to free jazz. In bed I worked for his pleasure, I didn't ask for mine and he didn't care. Often a little feverish, he was always saying, I feel weak, and wouldn't come to the studio for days. I was exhausted.

On a holiday trip in 1989 I had my first panic attack. At junctions the car made a noise like a heartbeat and the oleanders in the central reservation swayed in the wake of the articulated lorries. I'm dying, I whispered, more to myself than anyone else. The cork had popped on the despair

I hadn't known was within me. It had been simmering in the blindness of my heart. It had summoned me to make sense of it, in a flash of incandescent tarmac.

My mother is a river.

Her fine dark hair was a river, split by the current to run along the sides of her face, falling in waves over her breast. She combed it every night, after the long day's work. She'd walk singing, the river fluttering in the wind, but only at times, usually it was gathered in a bun. When she turned thirty she cut it off forever, it became insignificant, practical.

It used to be a stream. There was one not far from her home and on calm summer nights she liked to hear it burble through the open window, when the dogs fell silent.

She's a river of salvaged old memories, retold to all and sundry. She holds tight, lest her story burst into flames. Not many memories left, now. I replace them, I'm her scribe.

My mother was a river of words, only everyday platitudes now. How tall Giovanni is, a stitch in time saves nine, how cold it is this morning. On the phone she always asks me where I am. Knowing I'm at work reassures her. It has been the measure of her life.

She's a dried-up river, a blizzard of poplar flakes blowing over her. The rocks cast their shadows on the bleached, broken bed. Here and there a few puddles still, the water stagnant, murky, insects skimming the surface.

It smells of death.

Inevitable the encounter with fire, for the most fragile of your sisters. Serafina lit it before any portent of the coming dawn had begun to seep through the east-facing window. She swept the ashes and arranged firewood in the hearth as soon as she got up. She'd had to get up earlier than usual that day, there was an important job ahead.

After breakfast, your mother suspended a large copper cauldron over the flames from a chain on an iron hook, and filled it with water, rancid lard and flakes of caustic soda. Mind out of the way, as usual. A bucket of cold water had been placed nearby: a little would be poured in at intervals to soothe the boiling mixture. It was about to boil when Fioravante called from the stable in his most imperious tone and in two steps she was at the doorway to ask what's the matter. Clarice took advantage to get closer to watch, just as the mixture was rising and boiling over. She caught it full in the face, betrayed by the bubbling soda. She was eight years old and curious about the thick yellow liquid that grew as if by magic. Behind her young Nives screamed and screamed, clutching her hair. She didn't speak for a week, and no one could console her.

The traditional application of olive oil on the cooked skin made it worse, frying it, as the doctor would tell you later. The water from the bucket would have done the job, but who could have known. For the grace of St Lucia, according to the neighbours, the scalded child's sight was saved, but she would forever see through two slits in a pitifully disfigured face.

Serafina never forgave herself. No more homemade soap, relatives and neighbours would bring it to her already set and cut into pieces.

All her life Clarice has sought shadows and darkness, let her hair cover her face, kept her head down. She spoke rarely, to avoid attracting attention, and wore brown so as to melt into the background. When she was a girl she never asked for new clothes, or shoes. She admired her sisters, but without envy, through the goodness of her heart. Let's get it for Valkiria, should her mother decide to buy her some material for a skirt, you know how much it means to her. She wanted to go with you to the village, she wanted to disappear; to be there, but invisible.

The year she spent with us, when we moved to Atri, I shared a bed with her. She'd always sleep with her back to me, perhaps so she wouldn't scare me if I were to wake up suddenly. The way she smelled reminded me of fresh milk, it sweetened my dreams.

After she returned home, she'd visit every month. She married, late but she did marry, a widower in Mutignano, met during one of those visits. She disproved the grim prophecies of your spiteful moments. A mild man, a little older. He was fond of her and she devoted herself unsparingly to his son from his first wife. She might have yearned for children, but didn't want any. She felt unworthy of being a mother, because of that lack of beauty, as if it had been her choice. She never complained of her fate, she accepted it, in silent penance for a sin only she was aware of.

Her most tender affections went to those born to others, nieces, nephews and stepson.

You, on the other hand, wanted lots of children but Cesare didn't, and was always very careful to avoid them. Only the one, he said, she must get an education. We can't afford more.

Today you're sitting like a proper little old lady. That's not true. You'll bury us all, you come from a long-lived family. What's Granddad Fioravante got to do with that? He did die at 68, but it was his heart that let him down. The head for you, okay, but it's only your memory. When you get nervous you forget things; when you're calm you don't miss much. Distant memories remain, while recent ones struggle to imprint.

As with wheat: the store is safe, but a malevolent storm will shake the grains off the crisp heaves ready for harvest, and scatter them all over the field. That happened so many times, and instead of harvesting ten, we only managed seven or five. So are memories: if something disturbs them before they're stored they too can be lost. Stored grain can also rot, I didn't know that. I understand, with a trace of damp it gets warmer, and the little black bugs take hold.

It's Dad who makes you forget things, you're right, when he gets cross with you. Sometimes you feel you could just tell him where to get off and come and stay with us. Pietro's lovely, of course, but you'd be lonely when we're at work or at school. Pietro doesn't go any more, Giovanni does, he's in year five. You can barely believe it, it feels like he was born yesterday and he's ten already. Me? Forty-seven. I can't have another one now. I did want to, before, but it just didn't come. It is better when you're younger, I know, but I count myself lucky to have had Giovanni. And I want to live a long time, to watch him live his life.

You've undone your crochet, I see. It couldn't be turned into anything. Let's have a look at some of the older magazines to find a simpler pattern. The tablecloth with two rose branches doesn't seem that simple, the doily does, though, and it's pretty. I'll help you, I'll be your secretary. Start a ninety-stitch chain. Don't worry, I'll count them for you later, I'll prepare the pasta now. You have the sauce ready, I'll taste it.

There's a saucepan on the burner with a mismatched lid. It contains two garlic cloves fried in olive oil. I look over at her concentrating on the thread, she must have started to cook and then forgotten. I turn the gas on and start again with that lonely garlic, for a moment I fear embarrassing her with the sauce she had intended to prepare. But she's counting, mouthing the numbers. She seems happy. She's forgotten the sauce and me, two metres away across the tiles. She sings softly to herself. I wait for the first bubbles to break the surface and turn the flame down. I sit next to her again, I bend over her hands to check. Our heads bang together, we laugh.

One hundred and three, I'll unravel a few. Here. Go back seven stitches and then do a double crochet, three chain stitches and carry on like that. Don't worry, it's not difficult, I'll help you step by step. Finish this round for now.

Pietro alarmed you. A theatre actor, with no timetable, no harvest or salary, no apparent sacrifice. And he was shy, he hardly ever spoke, if he said anything nobody noticed. It took years for his silences to touch you. A while ago Dad admitted: he's the best out of all of us. One Sunday you came to one of his shows, Cesare enjoyed it, you fell asleep. Really. Too tired, it was the month for making hay. Don't worry, Pietro didn't see you. Let's cook something together for him, if you like, he'll come later with Giovanni. Perhaps you want him to forgive you.

But he's been my only free man. Out of the modest collection of boyfriends I paraded for Esperina as living proof I was worthy of love. Prisoner of a blind game, I took them to her, all so different from one another, to demonstrate once and for all how wrong she'd been not to love me enough. Look, they all want me. I spent years telling her.

Pietro felt dangerous to me, I couldn't control him. I was scared, without the need to run for cover. I could manage the fear. Alone in the little country house I was renting, with a willow at the front, I'd wait for him in the afternoon, in the kitchen, in my uncertainty. My senses were so taut, sharpened by desire, that I would first hear the engine of his car as he took the bend at the foot of the hill, then the gear change in readiness for the climb, first, second and third. I'd run to meet him by the willow, throwing caution to the wind. I had lost myself in an unimaginable love.

Even now, when it rains at night, I lie awake and listen to the pummelling of the road, the roof opposite, the window panes if it's windy. Then I delight in my house and him at my side, sleeping. Perhaps the rain falls inside his dreams. I hover near his face, witnessing his breathing. With a deviated septum, turbinate hypertrophy, and obstructed passages, the air whistles in search of a way through, it stops, restarts, accelerates, before easing off. I hear it, spur it on where it struggles most, I hold my breath if it stops, we begin again together.

How hard he works at night to stay alive. And I, while he sleeps unaware, steal his exhaling breath. This strange, precious companion, that I'm always at risk of losing, who's only a little bit mine.

Pietro isn't enough for you. You want me to tell you about the night Giovanni came. He made us wait, didn't he?

When the time was up, more days went by and still he wouldn't be born. I counted, one, two, three, one week, and more. I wasn't impatient, I savoured the anticipation. Before we've used up the white soap we wash our hands with, or the salt still in the packet, or before I need to cut my nails again, I thought, he'll come before that. You'd call at lunchtime and dinnertime, ask without even greeting me: any news?

The evening of the winter solstice my waters broke and off we went to the hospital. Sleet lashed the car windows, slowing us down. You two arrived when I was about to be wheeled into the delivery room; I waved at you. I noticed, you know, that you were about to cry.

After the labour, the music my son made reached me from the depths of my newly torn flesh: a cry, a breath, suction, and yet I couldn't see him. I asked where is he, and they laid him down by my head, already wrapped in a cloth, a little gasping being, damp and alive. He was desperately sucking on his left fist. I cried, I laughed, I don't know, Pietro was there, his hands on my cheeks and my sweaty hair. We were in the presence of our child.

Beyond the corridor and the opaque glass partition, a blue light flashed intermittently for you. When you got to see him he was already in his favourite position: curled-up legs, bum in the air and finger in his mouth. His big open eyes surprised you, once upon a time newborns kept their eyes closed even when awake, like the young of rabbits and cats, Dad recalled.

You didn't want to leave us, you stayed with me in room number five. My nightshirt was stained with blood, never mind you said, no need to change it, because I was trembling, with cold and with joy. Then you spread a blanket on the corner armchair, the tiredness of the day descending upon you. I didn't sleep all night, your breathing in harmony with that of the other new mum. I sensed, outside, the soft sound of an extraordinary event: forty centimetres of snow would fall that night. I waited for Giovanni to be brought to me. You weren't sleeping either, from the bed I felt you relaxed, alert. Every now and then you'd come near me to feel my forehead with your hand, testing for fever, as you would a little girl. I could see your broad shape move in the partial darkness.

At six they restored my child to me, I was exhausted by the separation. We watched him together under the neon light. The long stay inside of me, while the liquid was drying out around him, had given him the dry skin of a little old man, the surface flaking into minute transparent leaves. Petals, that's what they looked like, and observing the skin and the gestures of his tapered hands, I've given birth to my grandfather, I whispered to you. He looked like

135

his great-grandfather Rocco, who'd passed away a few days after Giovanni's conception.

Let's go to the hairdresser's today. To Lina's, as usual.

I liked your long hair, I would watch at sunset while you worked on it in your bedroom, by the window overlooking the wood. You'd be standing, moving in the mirror as you talked to me. The bun undone, you'd unravel the plait, the black river escaping down your back. It was a river, I swear, that you combed strand by strand, your head slightly bent to make the movement easier on your arm. I stared at you open-mouthed, admiring your treasure and how you cared for it. It was the only time of the day you would lose your briskness and grit, and the slow motion would soothe me to sleep.

Later, I'd sneak into your bed and bury my face and nose in it, letting strands of it slide through my fingers like silk thread. Once, when I was older, I dreamed your hair was black sugar candy, which I was slowly eating. No, you didn't go bald, it was never all gone. A strange dream, it's true.

Nearly all photographs show you with your hair done up. But look at this one, my favourite, the light falling sideways on your face, just a hint of a smile. A wave-like band caresses your cheek, rests on your shoulder, then slides down your breast, a dark and shining veil. The posed shots I don't like, here's one, standing to attention with startled eyes.

Or a tree.

She had high branches, I couldn't reach. She'd clothe herself with flowers as violet as her name, and me standing there, admiring from a proper distance. They smelled sweet. Some would fly in the wind, I could pick them up and sniff them closely. I would arrange the freshest one in my hair, behind my ear. I've appraised the texture of the petals between my thumb and my index finger.

Later, fruits would grow. The trunk was smooth, without holds for hands and feet. I've scraped my knees without ever managing to climb it. I'd jump up in the useless effort to grab something. In the end I remained on the ground, disappointed. Waiting, still. For the fall of an overripe fruit to bite into, careful to avoid the rot. Or I'd bite the rot off and spit it out, just so that I could linger in the enjoyment of whatever good was left.

My mother was a tree. I've had her shade.

My mother was a small, stumpy butterfly, *Hesperia*, with short wings and twitching flight. I used to dream of being able to touch her humble beauty. She was the beginning of all my longings, the mother of every loneliness.

One night I went to bed certain I'd never wake up. My heart had missed a beat, a sign that it was going to stop in my sleep. The foreboding was so strong that it must surely come to pass. Having had a last drink of water in the kitchen, I washed and upturned the glass to drain it. I took my clothes off, resting them carefully folded on the chair next to the bed, except my socks, left hanging over the back. I told my mother I was about to die, that my heart was missing beats. She told me not to talk nonsense and goodnight. Could I sleep in the big bed next to her? No, I could not.

Then, off I went under my sheets, covering my head, trembling with cold and fear. I breathed with my mouth open so the steam would warm me. Later, with the sheets up to my neck, I recited my last prayers, picturing the following day.

The little girl unresponsive to her calls, the exasperated mother trying to shake her awake, the terrible discovery of the body already cold and stiff. Ah the screams, my mother's agony. She'd pull her beautiful hair, screaming to those who'd rushed over, she told me, I didn't believe her. I wouldn't let her sleep next to us one last time. She left everything in order, the poor thing, look, the clothes folded on the chair, the socks over the back, the glass she last used upturned on the drainer, as she was taught. When I think of it, she did seem sad yesterday, lost in thought, and I never paid attention because I didn't have time.

At the climax of the scene my eyes would sting, my throat tighten. Then the hot and silent tears, running into the coils of my ears, wetting my hair, my pillow. I cried because she would cry for me. I slipped from compassion into a damp and comforted sleep. She'd withheld herself to the extreme. Tomorrow I would have all of her pain.

My mother's hand had not been able to hold me together while I broke into pieces, she didn't hear me crack, unaware of the world inside me. That night I dreamed I was clotted milk, fresh cheese she was squeezing. She wasn't able to comfort her child's anxieties. They developed into panic attacks, nightmares and, still to this day, slight discomfort.

That became my fantasy, every night. In the morning I'd wake up, alive and disappointed. I hadn't been able to get her attention by dying. I'd pull myself together as best I could, put on the clothes folded on the chair, the socks from over the back.

I was crazy about dolls, do you remember? I'd get them from my aunts as gifts. One was perhaps fifty or sixty centimetres high, of hard plastic, but the arms, legs and head could turn. A little unsettling, her blue gaze glassy and fixed, topped by jet-black hair. The dolls only had one dress each and I wanted to change them, so you helped me crochet skirts and tops. We found wool remnants and you taught me how. I was absorbed with playing the little mother and never wavered. Before going to bed, I'd cover them with a scarf made of many colours, kiss and cuddle them, and sing them to sleep. Practising for motherhood, you say. I don't think so. I never worked the thread again after I grew up.

The orderly in the bib apron escorts me to the room. I say good evening and approach a bed with the sides up. The voice behind me diligently warns me that the patient will not respond, he doesn't speak, doesn't chew, liquids only, therefore it's better to remove any remaining teeth, they are broken and sometimes cut the tongue. She leaves me with Orazio.

His eyes have an unusual colour, an unnatural shade of blue veiled by cataracts, they nearly glow in the inadequate grey light. Perhaps he can't see any more, and doesn't even know it. Under his cheekbones the skin is hollowed, and so are his lips, half-open, stretched a little over the few remaining rotten teeth. His mouth is a black hole, exhaling a musty smell, not bad enough to stink, more like a swamp. Gurgles rise from his gut.

The bones have taken over his face, you can tell what his skull will look like, under the fragile skin. The old man's neck, an Adam's apple resting on a bundle of spent muscles leaning on the three pillows that hold his back slightly raised.

I call him repeatedly, to give myself time to believe what I've been told. I find myself studying him, looking for my mother's tomorrow. He too is a moon of sorrows.

A flutter of nausea in my stomach, the desire to flee. I must remember that my friend Paola asked me to come today; her dentist is coming to pull her father's teeth and she might not get here in time, she's on shift at the factory.

I'm startled when a weak moan escapes this obliterated creature. I stroke his forehead with my fingertips and think back to what he was like. This is how the dentist finds us when the bib apron escorts him in. She casually hands me a pair of gloves, if you want you can help the doctor, then turns on her white heels and goes out of the door. He calmly lays a surgical cloth over the small table at the foot of the bed, where the meals are served, then lines up pliers and levers, a syringe. I reply to his questions on Orazio's condition, he injects him with anaesthetic. The moan is repeated and the doctor lifts his head questioningly, it's okay, I reassure him. A nod from him is enough for me to understand I need to keep his mouth open with my hands. At the first attempt of extraction the face contracts into a grimace, the dentist stops, we look confused at each other over the bed. In that instant Paola arrives, out of breath. She reassures us, her father no longer understands if he's in pain. How do you know, I nearly shout. Pinch him, hard, and see if he responds at all, she challenges me.

I could go but stay instead, rapt. Will he pull the root from the gum with that tool, I ask. No, from the bone, he answers mildly amused. When he's done he shows us the small stumps held between the claws of the pliers, only a little blood at the very tip. He sets them down on the cloth and carefully wraps up his tools. He's done, goodbye. My friend speaks to her father, calling him by his name. I notice a figurine on the bedside table, his grandchildren must have brought it. I kiss Paola on her cheeks and him on his forehead. I run away through a foul-smelling corridor, a sweltering hall, vaguely human bent-over shapes, blaring television, a lino-covered floor, some of the edges raised, the marble staircase at the entrance, and all that pain unravelling inside.

I run home and spend an age washing my hands. A tight hug to a surprised Giovanni, let's go and see Granny, I say.

Granddad died at dawn on the hottest day of June, the first day of my final exams. I wasn't told that morning, you didn't want to upset me. I had guessed something was wrong, you'd stayed over to sleep at your mother's.

Dad came to pick me up after my Italian test, he was waiting for me, looking sombre. Fioravante is no more, he said. We started to walk side by side, in silence. After the first few steps he swapped places with me; when he walks with someone my father always has to be on the left. Like cows pulling the plough, you can't swap them over.

We reached the house in Valle Medoro, built by Granddad when he too left the mountains. Old by then, he'd known the fertile land of the hills and Nives' children, his youngest grandchildren. And also the sticky sweetness of black grapes, the reddening of the pomegranates that drains bitterness from the grains inside, the pruning of olive trees. Over the years he became a knotty, gnarled trunk himself, the remaining hair like olive leaves, turning to grey confetti when upset by the wind.

I saw you first in the dimly lit corridor. You put your arms around my shoulders whispering, come, he's gone to heaven. Then the aunts, leaning against the wall in a row. My coming had rekindled their tears. Come, come, they murmured wringing their hands.

Granddad lay on the traditional counterpane, on the big bed. His handlebar moustache had been carefully trimmed, who knows who'd done it, Dad perhaps, with the small scissors he used for his, God help you if you touched them. He looked remote, at peace, his face diffused with the familiar charisma. He was covered by a white tulle net, a tenacious fly landing on it again and again, between his nose and mouth. Serafina on a chair next to the bed, mournful, collected. She'd sent all her daughters out of the room when she knew I was coming. She was already dressed in black, with the Virgin Mary gold medallion sparkling on her top, a handkerchief to wipe a tear held in her fist, dropped in her lap. She stood up to wave off the fly. I sat on the other side and we spoke to each other with our eyes, before watching over her man for a long time. I would wave off the fly. At one point she asked me to draw the sign of the cross over him. I said no and instead laid my hand on his, intertwined on his chest. We sat there for a time, then I briefly moved the veil to kiss his forehead. It felt cold and hard, dry in that incessant heat.

Later, other people came by, and then the undertakers. I hid in the cellar, curled up in a dark corner, breathing in the old familiar smells of Granddad's provisions. A fine golden dust was suspended in the little light that filtered from the door left ajar. I heard the light tap of teardrops on the brick floor, I looked through the lens of my tears.

When it was time for the funeral, Dad knew where to find me. He called softly from outside the door.

No car for the last stretch of road to the cemetery, we walked under the pines, crunching gravel underfoot, playing hide and seek with the sun. Fioravante would have wanted it that way. We breathed in the exhaust fumes of the hearse. At the same time, my school friends would be folding mathematical formulas into minute concertinas, to hide in their pockets for the maths test the following day.

The municipal gravedigger worked in front of us to inter Granddad, with noises of shovel sinking into cement, trowel laying on, bricks falling. I felt the hammer strike straight into my heart, enervating.

In October of the same year it was the other Viola's turn, Abele. Of course I remember your paternal uncle, he looked just like Yogi Bear. Fioravante thought him a little simple, big and thick, he'd say in jest. His parents had never come to terms with that good-natured, feeble son of theirs, prone to fat and debt. It was debt that bought him what his much cleverer brother never had, the means of transporting men and medium-sized beasts: an Apecar pick-up. He cared for it and kept it as clean as it was on the day he first got it. It was one of those rounded models, of an indefinable blue-grey colour; from the front it looked like a tabby hen.

The Apecar, with those little convergent wheels, would turn upside down at every opportunity, rounding a bend, on ice, down steep slopes. You have to be careful when distributing the load, it overturns more easily if it's not balanced. Uncle Abele tipped over lots of times, it's true.

He and Palmira, his wife, would squeeze into the cabin, he digging his elbow into her side when going round a bend. In their Sunday best, they'd go shopping down in the village. Put it on the tab, she'd say to the shopkeeper, and they'd go back to pay the bill after the Easter lambing, or harvest, months later, even. I know, Granddad never did that, he'd rather starve. Yes, I know, you never went hungry.

Uncle wouldn't leave his Apecar outside, he kept it in the barn, dry under cover. He was cheerful and talkative when driving, he'd shout above the engine noise and wave his arms around, perilously letting go of the handlebars. I didn't ride on it often, I liked it but was afraid of turning over, I'd lean to one side on the bends to compensate for the centrifugal force and he'd laugh, yeah right, you barely weigh ten kilos.

He died crashing that Apecar. His children arranged for the broken tricycle to be returned home, as he would've wanted. One side was intact, and Aunt Palmira had the other, the mangled side, turned against the wall of the barn so she'd never see it again. I went to see her a few days later and stayed into the evening. Valanga, the Abruzzi sheepdog of the family, would spend all his time lying on the ground by the front wheel and hadn't eaten since. I got close, turned the sticky handle, breathed in deeply. Every car has a different smell, which matures over the years, like wine. Here was the smell of the Apecar, my uncle's smell: stale armpits, hair, shoes, a memory of his breath. There on the seat the imprint of the driver's weight and at its side, smaller, that of his passenger. The old grey leatherette, hardened and finely cracked, a deserted land.

I sat lightly on my aunt's seat. The cold went through my skirt to my legs. Later, the windows steamed up with my body heat. I rolled one down, to see outside. As soon as I closed it, the grey egg reformed around me. I sat there for a long time thinking about Uncle Abele. When I got out it was nearly dark in the barn. At my first step my ankle found the dog's snout.

How many ghosts I'm bringing back. So strong when alive, with the passing of time they become powerless figurines, almost pitiful. They committed the sin of leaving before us.

My mother was a musical instrument, her body a viola, the chords humming when she sang with her mouth closed.

I'm tired of her. Of carrying her mark through my life. I haven't managed to free myself. I let her invade me, still. Infest me. I react to her and waste my time. I keep going round and round without finding a way to escape her orbit towards new worlds. I'm getting old, without growing up.

She moves in dark chambers. From time to time she sees me, from afar. Again, she picks up her tape measure and holds it up to me. As usual, I don't measure up. She tries another tack. The hair I never comb. The posture of a beaten dog, sit up straight. She's always said that to me. I look at her like a dog looks at the stick, I give up trying to bite. I grind my teeth.

A few days in Pompeii, Sorrento. Giovanni drinks stall-bought lemonade, they call it freshly squeezed juice here. The pedlar outside the hotel tries to sell him a Napoli T-shirt, he resists the pressure and buys an Inter Milan cap for Cesare instead. I tell him that my parents only ever travelled for work, allowing themselves the occasional visit to distant relatives. He wants to know where, and when, and who. He warms to the subject, feeling sorry for his grandparents. To him, holidays are ordinary, they're for everyone. He doesn't know the cost of normality, the guilt I feel towards my mother. She brought me up to believe in sacrifice, the alarm set for seven even when there was no school, so I wouldn't get used to doing nothing. She'd say the fresh morning air was good for me.

I disobeyed, and I feel guilty for every gratuitous happiness. For every time I don't have to sweat blood over it. I measure the extent of my betrayal.

The apron looks good on you, Giovanni got it for you in Pompeii, we went for the long May Day weekend. Pompeii, you know, the Vesuvius eruption. No, don't worry, it's not erupting any more. I'd mentioned it to Dad, perhaps he forgot to tell you. Yes, Pompeii. I know you studied it at school, I remember you telling me about the petrified bodies.

You two could go. Don't say you're too old, you're just not used to it. Many years ago the train did take you to Aunt Lucianella, who had emigrated to Piedmont. Cesare's sister, that's right. But you weren't really going on holiday, just giving in to invitations that bordered on threatening. And Vercelli isn't exactly a holiday resort, especially late in the autumn, like that time. It was the best time to leave home, after sowing; Uncle Remo could see to the animals for a few days, he was no longer working in Switzerland by then. No, I didn't, I went to hers one Christmas, I remember the road stretching ahead, the damp horizon resting on the car bonnet, until we reached the large farmstead, lonely in the rice fields.

Uncle Marcello operated the machines on the land, Aunt kept house for the owners. There, too, a mother died, of distraction. The woman of the house had gone to town shopping, didn't come back at lunchtime. In the shops she normally visited, nobody knew a thing. They worked their way backwards, slowly, on the tarmac stretched tight, no sign of braking or anything. After searching for several hours, there she was in the fog, her face on the twisted wheel, her mouth and eyes open. The incredulous husband demanded an autopsy, but they found nothing. Uncle still says that it's impossible to go off the road on such a level stretch. He says that the greyness infiltrated her heart and she must have forgotten to live. He'd tell of those low, everlasting clouds, a migrant come home to the light of the south, and shake his head.

Aunt brought up the woman's children and came to terms with her own grief. She'd lost her mother as a young girl, remember? Maria Concetta, your mother-in-law and aunt, my gran and Cesare's much-missed mother.

I went off on a tangent, we were talking about your holiday in Vercelli. I beg your pardon, it wasn't a holiday. From that place, ugly though not devoid of its own secret appeal, you went on to the Aosta Valley, sending postcards from Courmayeur and others with pictures of Mont Blanc.

Our mountains, you said on your return, in winter they look like chunks of bread with curd on top, in the north of Italy the peaks are too sharp, they're scary. You did help Aunt a little, of course, you could not be idle. On the last night she served a fondue and you, always proud of eating anything, anything and everything, you couldn't manage to get it down. You made do with mandarins; the fondue's a one-course meal, there was nothing for afters.

Let's get lunch ready, I've bought handmade tagliatelle. No, you know I can't make them, I bought them at the fresh pasta shop. As we chat we can shell the broad beans Dad picked this morning. So fresh, after just one day they'll have lost their flavour. I've brought some peas as well, shelling them relaxes me. Careful, pods here and kernels there, on that plate. I sauté a thinly sliced new onion in the oil and add the vegetables, then cubed pancetta from the famous pig, the one Dad slaughtered at the beginning of the year. In the meantime I'll drain the tagliatelle al dente, reserving a little of the cooking water. Once flavoured with the sauce, let's keep them covered for a few minutes, they'll be tastier that way. Then we can add a little chilli pepper to our plate.

She lies with a face of hard wax, mouth twisted in the usual sneer of disapproval. On her chest the hands are crossed in a little mound of dry twigs. I watch over her in the yellow light of the candles, the air's heavy with the scent of wilted flowers. I stare at them and, as if provoked by my gaze, a petal falls with a soft sound. I stand up and put my ear to her mouth, perhaps life evaporates from her still. I sit down again, motionless but for my breath.

She sits up with a jerk, her bust rotates and launches in my direction. I receive the full force of her slap on my face. She lies down again like a mechanical doll. The burning on my cheek is a red sun, with five rays.

My mother's rings would wake me, on non-working days. For her it was a working day like the others, she'd been up since five so she saw nothing strange in phoning me at seven thirty. It would enrage me, every time.

Some Sundays now she wakes me up with a dream. It's a sign, she wants me with her. I go to her before Giovanni and Pietro get up. I'll come back later and we'll have the day to ourselves.

The wind blows. The slap was the shutter banging.

It won't last long, it's a yellow and hopeless wind, escaped by chance from a door in the mountains. The wood's already pulling it back to itself, like a disobedient child. I like it when it stops, the countryside gives a sigh of relief and slowly recovers from its lethargy. The dishevelled plants return to their habitual posture, the ruffled leaves rotate on their stalks, facing the sun. You can hear it, the last few gusts are so weak. Granddad Rocco taught me. To read the clouds, the wind. I'd stand next to him on the balcony and in a loud clear voice he'd explain the sunset to me, predicting what the weather would be the next day. Knowing nothing of cardinal points, he'd use mountains and hills for reference. When the clouds behind Colle Mancino turned black there was no escape; even if not quite dry yet the hay would have to be gathered before dawn and certain rain. He'd study the whole sky, the grouping of clouds, their shapes and colours. Of the wind, the origin and strength. He'd cross-reference the information gathered with temperature, humidity and approximate statistics of atmospheric events of the past. He was much better than Bernacca and all his education.

Fabrizio, his grandson, was his favourite, but he softened towards me when he was older. He'd be surprised that every day someone would look for me at the studio, could it be possible? I was the only one allowed to cut his nails, with his hand already stretched out he'd urge me not to cut too close, or he'd feel the cold on his fingertips.

I prefer the hearthstone to the chair. I don't know why we sit here even when the weather's warm and there is no fire.

We don't need to light it, it's nearly summer. I'll rest my head on your legs, if you don't mind. When I was little you couldn't sit down for a minute without me putting my face in your lap. I'd seek the scent of your skirt, a blend of all your tasks, it gave off head and tail notes like an exquisite perfume. It smelled green after working in the alfalfa field.

Now I can tell her everything about us, without mercy. She'd forget later. It would be but a fleeting wound. I fantasise about it, but I can't find the courage to be so cowardly.

I get there as an exhausted sunset dives beyond the outline of the Sleeping Giant. The little gate squeaks the same way it did when Artibano, the blacksmith, mounted it halfway through the seventies, it goes click when it closes. I'm not going up, I sit on a step and rest my head against a wall warmed by the recently departed sun. I hear my mother moving a chair in the kitchen.

I've studied, I've read sitting on these steps, in between dealing with domestic chores. Here I prepared for the oral exams of the summer session, here I studied history of art. Between one page and the next I would stare up at the sky, losing myself in impenetrable minutiae, the adventures of clouds a strain on my neck.

I sniff the white stone, it has a good smell of past rain. My mother finds me like this, my head on the marble.

No, I'm not feeling unwell, don't worry. I'd dropped a coin. Sit here with me for a moment, look, what a beautiful evening. All the stars are coming out. And a few fireflies, look. I love fireflies. When you were little, you were told not to hold them in your cupped hands, that you'd get warts that way. The same if you counted stars pointing with your finger. No, I wasn't there, I learned that a long time after, from you.

Now you want me to start again from the beginning. I'll start right away, that's what I'm here for.

You are Esperina Viola, my mother. Like a violet, you were born on 25th March 1942, in a house on the border between the districts of Colledara and Tossicia. You are the child of a military leave, and so were some of your sisters.

I'm not graceful, nor light-hearted. I'm tethered to the ground, teeth grinding on the links of my chain. My mother, that's what I've labelled every limit. I have charged her with the imperfection of my flight. She's been my excuse. She's the cause, and the reason.

My mother is a tree. In her shade I have absolved myself. It's shrivelling, the shade too shrinks away. Soon I'll be exposed.

It's true: nothing bad ever happens to thieves and robbers, bad things only happen to good people. There is no room for good people on this earth.

Your uncle is a scoundrel, he thinks only of himself and his land, while your father breaks his back helping everybody else. He never talks to me, he gives me dirty looks. I heard him say to his wife that I'm crazy.

Why, isn't Diamante the youngest? Who is then? Clorinda? It can't be, Clorinda's dead, poor thing, it must be Clarice. Which one was born after me? Diamante?

Hasn't Giovanni grown. I was afraid he'd be short, like me.

Thank goodness you've come, an angel must've whispered in your ear.

ACKNOWLEDGEMENTS

To Raffaella Lops, my guiding angel.

Thank you to my parents for allowing me to study, it wasn't easy. And for a lot more besides.

To Laura Grignoli, who believed in my writing when I myself did not.

To all my friends, acquaintances and strangers who have helped me in various ways, in particular with information, photos and other useful material for my book. To Emanuela and Anna Lina Massimi who took me from dream to reality.

To Loretta Santini who has more than once, with the necessary courage and/or recklessness, taken a punt on a new writer hiding away in the Italian countryside. To her enthusiasm and the team she similarly enthused.

To my land, the Campo Imperatore upland, where crocuses announce spring by rising out of the last snow.

A clarification on the choice of the surname Viola, very common in Abruzzi and Italy: I chose it because it is the only one which represents a flower, a colour and a musical instrument. The story is fictitious and is not based on any Viola, either in the present or in the past.

LPA Services

LPA Services believe that every family should safeguard the resources they have created by ensuring key elements are put in place to support individual members who need care now or in later life and when it matters most.
A Lasting Power of Attorney (LPA) is a legal registered document that allows an individual to appoint people they trust to act on their behalf when required.
These can be used in circumstances such as loss of mental capacity, heart attack, stroke, accident, dementia, or for many other reasons.

Tel. 01795 503 184

www.lpaservices.co.uk

Terracotta Ristorante italiano

"A lovely little Italian restaurant hidden in Hythe High
Street, very friendly and efficient service, freshly real
cooked real Italian food at reasonable prices.
Well worth a visit" (Tripadvisor review)

22 High Street, Hythe, CT21 5AT

Tel. 01303 264888

http://cardinirestaurant.com/